# Martin W

Martin has been a social worker for over 30 years. He has also worked in the field of employment law. His interests include music, cookery, travel and running (more as a spectator than a participant nowadays). Martin, who is married with grown-up children, lives in the East Midlands with his wife, Janet and two dogs, Max and Tess. Martin has been nominated for the 'Social Worker of the Year' Award 2010.

This is dedicated to Janet without whose patience and support I'd never have finished it.

# Acknowledgements

I'd like to thank all those who offered encouragement for their assistance and support.

I am especially grateful to John and Phil McCauley, Malcolm Maloney, Graham Keal, Sridhar Gowda and Geraldine Rose, Anna Weinbren and Natasha Scott-Dunn, Zuza Vrbova and Andrew Jackson. I would also like to record my appreciation and thanks to my late father, Professor Ken Weinbren, whose medical knowledge and editing skills were invaluable in helping me to complete it.

Finally I have to acknowledge the help and wisdom of Ann Knight, whose wit and use of English inspired me to write a particular colourful character into the book. She knows which one.

# King Welfare

## Martin Weinbren

*To Toni
Best wishes
Martin W[einbren]*

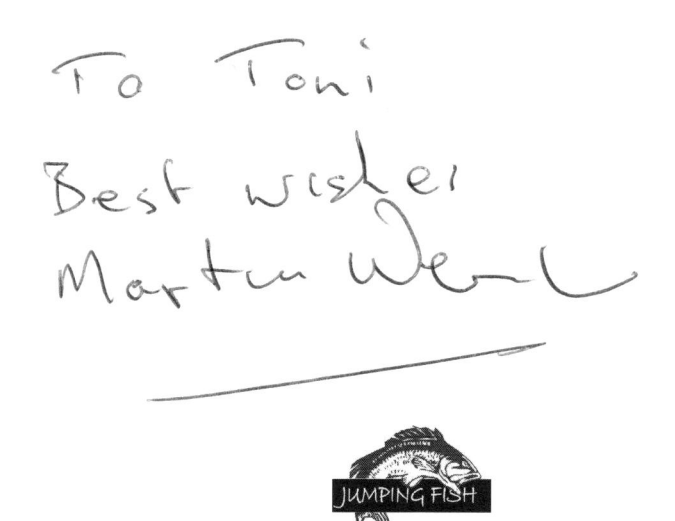

First published by Jumping Fish 2010

Copyright Martin Weinbren 2010

All rights reserved
The moral right of the author has been asserted

Cover Design Ian Orange

Printed in England

No part of this publication may be reproduced, stored in a retrieval system, or transmitted, in any form or by any means, electronic, mechanical, photocopying, recording or otherwise, without the prior permission of the publishers.

A CIP catalogue record for this book is available from the British Library

This book is a work of fiction. Names, characters, places and incidents are either a product of the author's imagination or are used fictitiously. Any resemblance to actual people living or dead, events or situations is entirely coincidental.

ISBN: 978-1-907219-18-4

Jumping Fish
An imprint of Peak Platform Limited UK
www.peakplatform.com

# One

Fountain Medical Centre was packed. Sarah Moss waited by the door, clearly concerned about the amount of coughing in the waiting area. It was the sixteenth of February and her second visit of the month. She reached down to unclip Harley from his pram. Sarah was nineteen and knew she was attractive, with her shoulder-length light brown hair and slim size 10 figure, even after having had two children. 'Heroic', they called her. Helen, her Health Visitor was always telling Sarah what a Good Little Mum she is. Without thinking, Sarah kissed Harley's chubby little cheek and sniffed his head before sniffing the base of his tee-shirt and pulling a face. Short of things to look at, all eyes were on her.

'We'd better change your bum, my sweetheart,' she cooed at him, aware of her audience. 'We can't have you putting the Doctor off his coffee.' She put his anorak on the lower shelf of the pushchair, picked up his corduroy shoe, complete with Monsters Inc sock from the floor and conscious of the smiles among the other patients, scooped up a Pampers and Sudocrem pot from her bag and eased toward the Mother and Baby room.

Placing the five-month old on the table, she changed his nappy and then in a quick movement, leaned over him, placed her own shirt tail over his nose and mouth. He wriggled, struggling for breath. Some three minutes later, he stopped moving and she stepped back, tucking in her shirt. Putting her ear to his nose, she made sure the little figure had started to breathe again, then screamed, picked him up and rushed out into the waiting room.

'It's happened again,' she shrieked at an approaching nurse, 'It's happened again - he's had one of his fits.' Harley's face had turned a grey-blue colour. Nurse Eva Forbes took the child, moved quickly to a large cupboard and removing a small oxygen cylinder from it. She turned it on, putting the mouthpiece to the child's face. Slowly, the child's face turned pinker, as he woke up and started to cry. Sarah accepted the baby from the nurse and sat sobbing and cuddling him as several members of staff fussed around her offering cups of tea. As an elderly man came out from the consulting room, the Nurse went in and shortly afterwards, summoned Sarah who was still cuddling Harley.

*Apnoea Attack resulting in cyanotic episode*, Dr Sebastian Cruickshank wrote, turning to Sarah at the end of his examination of Harley. 'This is obviously very hard for you to cope with on your own - do you have any support at home?' Sarah sobbed and shook her head.

'Not just now,' she mumbled and pulling some crumpled toilet roll from her bag, dabbed at her eyes.

'How often do these occur?' Seb was in his fourth year out of Medical School. He'd been with Fountain Medical Centre just two of those, initially as a locum, after a spell as a House Physician at Lincoln Hospital.

*?Septal defect/possible nut allergy/laryngeal obstruction - Check U & Es, ref. Cardiologist, Allergy clinic. ?Lumbar Puncture. S/servs for support.* In Doctor's handwriting. Very neat, but absolutely unreadable and incomprehensible to the outside world.

'Once, maybe twice a week, or sometimes not for a whole month.' Sarah kept looking down.

'I'm going to send him for some tests - blood, heart and allergies. I'd also like to see if Social Services can give you some support. Okay? Keep him warm and call an ambulance or come back here at once if it's quicker should it happen again.'

The waiting patients greeted Sarah with quiet sympathetic smiles as she repacked the pram. *Brilliant Young Mum and nobody will ever know it has anything to do with my Special Hug,* she thought to herself as she left the surgery.

Nurse Eva watched through the window as Sarah left the surgery, a spring in her step. For a minute, a slight feeling of unease came over Eva. The fleeting thought passed and she returned to her notes.

# Two

On the same street, just four buildings down, in the Social Services office, Albert handed a grubby scrap of paper to Jake, a smart young man sitting opposite. CARBORRIBEL FITTASBORER it read at the top. Jacob Atkinson, in spite of all his experience over a couple of years as a duty social worker in several different offices, read it, but wasn't sure quite what to make of it the first time he saw it written. Albert Steggles was his name. And that's as much as he could write. He came to the office at least once a fortnight and asked for help to apply for a job. He always brought the form, asked to see the duty social worker and wanted to have a form filled in. It was his eyesight, so he said and he couldn't be doing with glasses. Of course, as the new worker to the team, Jake saw him.

'You've already filled part of the form in, then?'

'Ay, I thought I'd fill in the bits I could.'

CARBORRIBEL FITTASBORER. A Job Description. Printed beautifully. Tongue out the side of the mouth job. Jake had asked the team about Albert before going to see him. Albert lived on an allotment, they said, in a lean-to made out of old doors and corrugated tin he'd found in skips. Nobody had asked what he survived on. He was actually forty-two years of age but looked sixty, with teeth stained from years of smoking roll-ups.

'Put on the form Hard Worker. I'm a real grafter, me. Tell 'em I'll not let 'em down and I don't need much pay.' And he meant it.

Albert leaned forward and uncrossed his legs. Jake noticed his trousers, a pair of frayed flairs that could have been part of a C & A suit from 1970. The front of his left trainer was split into a smile. Jake suddenly felt self-conscious about his own appearance. He looked healthy. His twice-a-week sessions at the gym since college had filled out his six-foot-two frame and he made sure he had a sufficiently balanced diet to sustain his training routine. His Pierre Cardin shirt, Chinos and Timberland Loafers had probably cost more than this man would spend on clothing in his whole lifetime. Jake shifted uncomfortably, briefly lost for words. Albert gave a long sniff, followed by a swallow, then reached a foil pack of Old Holborn out of the pocket of his grubby cardigan and spread a tiny amount of it across a Rizla.

'Actually, I don't read ever so good.' Albert wheezed quietly and nodded. 'But I'm a bloody good worker. Tell'em. Tell'em I'll do owt.'

'If you don't find reading easy, how d'you do your shopping, how d'you cope with buses and the rest?' Jake was pondering as much to himself as to Albert. Imagine what you can't do without the written word. And where did CARBORRIBEL FITTASBORER come from? Long words. Or maybe not, when you think about it. Just lots of letters.

'Them pies in the flat blue and cream coloured tins. Them's what I like. And when you go to shops, you've got to ask for your 'baccy and papers. Them lasses in Co-op, they know me - it's Eh up Albert is it yer usual? Two packs'll do me a week.' Albert's index finger and thumb were a shiny golden colour. He looked hungry and worn out. His diet of boiled tinned pies and roll-ups hadn't done him any favours over the years.

DIPSW. Diploma in Social Work. Three years of theory-to-practice, risk assessments and cycles of abuse, with endless Americanisms, total political correctness and absolutely anti-oppressive practice. For what? Bloody Albert and his job applications.

Jake Atkinson was twenty-nine. He'd fallen into social work by mistake, as had many of his colleagues. Working as a wages clerk in a transport firm in Bulwell, he'd been bored one lunch time. Bulwell. Famous for nothing but its firework factory and slabthonic women. Certainly not a place for a gifted twenty-three year old to carve out a career of any sort. Reading through the local paper, he'd seen a vacancy for a social work assistant in Mansfield and just for something to do, he phoned them. Having filled in the application form, he had submitted it and to his surprise, ended up with a new career. Eighteen months later, he'd gone off to college, having been fortunate to secure a place on the qualification course. Now, two years down the road from graduating, he was still moving from one temporary social worker post to another. When you're happy to work in child protection, there's no shortage of jobs. Albert was an exception to the child care remit. The office dealt with him because no one wanted to turn him away. Jake looked again at the words CARBORRIBEL FITTASBORER written on the form.

'Your last job - the bit you've filled in - what was your exact job title again? I thought I'd just double check your spelling.' Gentle Jake, they called him at college because he never liked to hurt anyone's feelings.

'Driver's Mate, like I've wrote.' Problem solved. Quiet sigh of relief. Neither Jake nor anyone else would ever know or work out how Albert had copied letters from C. A. Roberts Engineering (Engine Rebore and Fitting Specialists) many years before. Albert certainly couldn't explain it.

'I'd spell it a little differently. Can I correct it?'

'Aye, you write it posh as you like.'

And so it went. Albert probably wouldn't get his job and Jake couldn't quite bring himself to discuss why with him.

They were interrupted by a knock on the door. Sue, the receptionist peered through the porthole of a window in the door. Jake motioned her in and she apologetically passed a yellow Post-it. On it was written 'HV - CP.' With a sinking feeling and promising to complete the form and post it for him, Jake wished Albert good luck with his job application and went through to the General Office where he had a desk for when it was his turn to have a day as Duty Social Worker.

'Which Health Visitor and what sort of Child Protection referral?'

'Helen Keal's on my phone. Will you take the call up in the Team room? I think it might be a bit iffy.' Sue's normally quiet voice dropped to a whisper. 'It's the Hegarty baby.'

The team room was an untidy mishmash of six teak-coloured desks and brown Hessian swivel-chairs. The walls were Elastoplast-pink, with uplighters like surgical dishes. Jake thought it had been arranged to enable everyone to avoid conversation with the rest of the team. He edged his way past Christine's shrine - a multi-coloured crocheted blanket covering her chair and photographs of some twenty or so children on a notice board. Chrissie was proud of those. Every one personally rescued by her for a more Christian life in the Care of the Local Authority. Some permanently institutionalised as a result. Chrissie had no fewer than three Godchildren on her caseload and prayed for them every night, in her Perthshire growl. She'd done her twenty-two years in the RAF as a clerical assistant. Senior Aircraft Woman Christine McBride had done her duty for Queen and Country and was still doing her duty for God. Always a McBride, but never a Bride, thought Jake. A kindly woman, but tight-fisted, a charisma bypass and strictly God squad.

As Jake sat to take his phone call, Chrissie turned.

'Albert alright today?'

Jake nodded and picked up the phone. Hegarty baby. A bit like a version of colic. One of the problems with being new is everyone else's knowledge of what you should be doing with clients they all know and problems you've never heard of. Taking a deep breath, he picked up the telephone.

'Hello, it's Jacob Atkinson, duty social worker. How can I help?' he began.

'It's Helen Keal, health visitor attached to Fountain Medical Centre. I've been to do the three month check on Stevie-Lee Hegarty this morning and to be honest, I'm... well I...' she broke off. 'This is confidential, isn't it? It's just I don't want her to know it's come from me. She trusts me and tells me things.' Jake reached for a referral form.

'I'm not sure that the family won't have to know eventually', he replied, quietly. They always seem to want to pass the buck without responsibility, he thought.

'Well I can't leave it - I'm worried because he's not responding too well and this morning - it might be nothing - but I thought he had a bit of a black eye.'

'Facial bruising', Jake murmured as he wrote it down. 'Can you be more specific for me please? Do you mean there was faint bruising or was a small part around his eye bruised?' He heard the health visitor start to sob at the other end of the telephone.

'I didn't mean to...' she tailed off, 'It's just I get so confused about what you're allowed to say nowadays.' It occurred to Jake that she had moved into the arena of Politically Correct Language.

'I think I'm probably able to pick up the background information from our files,' he said. 'Just give me an idea of when I'll catch them at home.' But the telephone had already been put down. 'Bollocks,' he muttered and turned round to find Chrissie glaring at him.

Before she could say anything about his language, the team door flew open and a tall broad man in his late forties briefly filled the doorway before making a theatrical entrance.

'Who d'you have to fuck round here to get a cup of coffee?'

'I'll make you one, Tom,' Chrissie responded to the fast deep cockney voice that had boomed its way into the room. Tom Davey was dressed in a suit jacket with tie and jeans. Twenty years qualified and forty-seven years old, he knew the area and its people well and on occasion was social worker to mothers who had been on his caseload as babies. He was the union Workplace Representative and as such was considered by some to be above criticism. Tom looked Chrissie up and down, pointedly.

'I'd rather make my own on second thoughts,' he replied, lumbering off towards the kitchen.

Jake found himself wondering about Albert and his job prospects as he drove up towards Thorpe Park to see Stevie-Lee, the Hegarty baby. The Police had agreed that he should visit initially without them, although it was normal procedure to visit jointly.

'Your Fifteen Pounds,' the radio announced, in a soothing, needy voice, 'can help save a child from suffering further abuse...' Jake changed the radio station. Your Fifteen Pounds will help fund expensive television and radio campaigns to make our organisation seem more important and put more work onto less important organisations, he thought. Jake had no sympathy for corporate radio begging, when all the voluntary agencies did was to call the Local Authority Children's Services and get them to do the visit. He found himself humming along to an old Doctor Hook song...*She was too young to fall in love and I was too young to know...* Jake turned the radio off.

Thorpe Park. Lovely name. Horrible estate to visit. Everyone wanted to move away from it. Up Stafford Crescent, right onto Worcester Drive. 1920s homes fit for heroes, Lloyd George had intended them to be. Now they made up the most unpleasant sink estate in the East Midlands. They hadn't been built to take a 'welcome'- sofa outside the front doors that not even the Alsatians would sit on. The social worker knocked at the door. A small pair of deep-brown eyes peered at him through an opened letterbox and a child's voice called through,

'Who is it?'

'Is your Mum in, please - I've come to talk with her.'

A man's voice bellowed from upstairs, 'If it's the club man, I'll pay him next week and if it's 'king welfare tell 'em to sod off.'

A woman opened the door.

'I'm Jacob Atkinson from Social Services. I've had a call about Stevie-Lee. May I come in, please?'

As Jake walked into the Hegarty household, his loafers made a slight tearing sound as they stuck to the carpet with each step. The house had a distinct smell of old body odour, new urine and sour milk.

'Marie Hegarty?' Jake began. She nodded. 'We've had a call about Stevie-Lee. I'm from Social Services and whenever we get any sort of report about a child who may be at risk, we have to…' He didn't finish the sentence as the door from the hallway to the lounge opened and a pair of angry eyes glared at him.

'What gives you the right to barge into my fucking house and question my fucking wife about my fucking children?' Jake turned to respond and found himself facing five foot of seething anger. L O V E on the right fingers, H A T E on the left and Fuck You tattooed in small letters on the neck. Tosser tattooed on his brain, thought Jake. Not a good idea to voice it, really.

It's at times like these that social workers are at their most vulnerable. He had checked the file before leaving the office and had noted visits had usually been done in pairs to this family. Jake felt decidedly nervous, but determined not to show it. He also didn't want to appear too threatening in case he prompted a violent response. He wished that one of his colleagues had had the good grace to forewarn him of this man's aggression. The problem is that although Roy Hegarty would likely get a prison sentence if he hit a social worker in the course of his duty, if that social worker defends himself, he could get the sack for unprofessional conduct. Being male and fit only makes you a more viable target.

'Section 47 Children Act 1989. That's what gives me the right. What I've got to do is check out the concerns we've had, hopefully with your help and co-operation.' Jake waited. He knew what the response would be.

'You've no need to have any concerns about any of my kids. Now just piss off back to your office. And tell your boss Frances Fucking Phillips she can piss off too.'

Jake lowered his voice and said quietly, 'I'm sorry, I can't do that. I've a job to do and one way or another it will be done. I want to see Stevie-Lee and the other children, I want to talk to you about our concerns and I want to assess where we go from there.' He waited a few seconds to see what response he would get. Silence. Time for the rehearsed lines. 'Whenever we get a call expressing concern about any child, it has to be checked out. This is what the law says. Sometimes it is done jointly by a social worker and a police officer and sometimes by one or the other. What we do is see the child, talk with the parents and check out whether the child is okay. If there needs to be a medical, we ask the parent to come with us for the child to be seen by a paediatrician. We also check up with all the agencies concerned. What you don't want us doing is going through the process behind your back, or being forced to barge in with a court order to take the child away because you won't let us see the child and we think you've got something to hide.'

As Jake paused, he glanced round the room. Newish decoration. Pale aubergine with gold stars, matching Edwardian border and Regency stripes below. More Argos than IKEA. There was something about the layout of the room which did not quite lend itself to trendy decoration. Twelve-foot by twelve-foot around a Parkray fire never looks like the adverts promise. The door frame, nicotine over white gloss, had dog bite marks at the base. Navy woodchip had probably seemed like a good idea at the time, but on the ceiling it gave the room a dark and dirty feel. Somehow the carpet had at some stage turned from liver and cream tufts to leatherette with a Velcro afterstep. The terracotta-tiled fireplace had two overfilled ashtrays and a half-filled coffee mug. There was a turd trapped by the hem of the curtain. Jake quietly tensed and wondered where the dog was. Marie hovered in the doorway, as Roy loudly huffed. As Jake watched, Roy Hegarty seemed to relax a little. Give them a chance to save face, he'd been taught, even if only a little. How do you accord them respect when they're so angry? The three-piece suite had been well used. Catalogue furniture tends to get past its best-before-date before it's paid for in such places, he mused.

'I'm not havin' the bastard filth in this house', Roy Hegarty barked. 'Coppers that is', he added for Jake's benefit. Good. He was softening, thought Jake.

'Will I be spelling that with a capital B and a capital F when I write my report, then?'

'Spell it 'ow yer 'king like.' Roy half smiled. Sorted.

'Let's see the baby then.' Roy glanced across at his wife and gave a barely discernible nod. Marie slipped out.

As Marie came back into the room, carrying the baby, she was followed by two toddlers in combat fatigues, one half a head taller than the other.

'This is Ricky and that one's Ryan,' Marie began, 'And them scratches on their faces is eczema and fighting,' she finished.

Jake turned and smiled. 'You don't really fight, a nice lad like you?' Ricky looked sideways at him out of big brown three-year-old doe-like eyes and glancing across at Marie, nodded slowly and said accusingly, 'I saw you through the letterbox.'

Marie sat and beckoned Jake to do the same. With some apprehension in case the sofa was wet, Jake sat and looked at the baby on Marie's knee.

'We had a report suggesting he might have some bruising round his eye.' Jake recalled the health visitor's wish to stay anonymous.

'It's that health visitor cow. I'll have bloody words with her.'

So much for anonymity, thought Jake, saying nothing in response as he turned to look at the baby. A fat pair of ruddy cheeks framed a runny nose and wet lower lip. Not a clean face. A bit like a young farmer. A very young farmer. He looked at Jake and burst into a gummy smile. There was some shadowing under the right eye.

'What's that?' Jake pointed. Marie leaned forward and putting the hem of her grubby apron into her mouth, proceeded to rub the baby's face with it. The 'bruise' transferred to the apron.

'I don't think we'll be having a child protection conference. You should get a letter telling you we won't be going any further with this one.'

Roy began, almost apologetically, 'I didn't...'

'We'll forget our earlier introduction, shall we?'

As Jake climbed back into his car, he realised the sofa had been wet.

Chrissie looked up from her desk as Jake walked back into the office.

'He's driven back from Thorpe Park, so he can't have left his car parked for too long.' She glanced across to Sally Beckett, sitting also facing the wall at the next desk. They all knew at least one family in Thorpe Park with an accomplished TWOC'er as one of its members. Taking Without Owner's Consent of a vehicle didn't count as a crime among many families up there. As long as you hadn't nicked it from on the Estate.

Sally turned. 'Hi, how's my pal Roy?'

Jake couldn't imagine anyone less likely to be Roy's pal. Sally's hair was a natural blonde and cut to perfection in an early Princess Diana style. Her fringe fell in a planned carefree way across her twenty-five year old forehead and her mascara was always applied to perfection. There was never an eyelash out of place and Lincoln City would be top of the Premier League before she ever let anyone see a run in her tights. During the summer months when she wore her Gucci sandals even her toenails looked manicured. Never polished. Far too vulgar.

Jake considered his reply to Sally for a couple of seconds. 'He had a message for me. Tattooed on his neck. You could say he wasn't a happy lad today. Decidedly unhappy, in fact. Questioned my child care credentials and my personal habits. I hadn't been told he was your pal. Is he?'

Sally gave a half smile, winked across at the next desk where Lakshmi Patel was seated and returned to her paperwork. Lakshmi, having looked up from her note-writing, half-offered a smile in return and went back to her writing.

Jake assembled the collection of papers from his in-tray, which was in the general office. Laying them out on his desk, he considered them one-by-one. Confirmation of verbal referrals from the Health Service, three new referrals allocated to him and some written-up file notes back from the typist.

This was how work was distributed in this team. Either a child protection investigation was picked up and followed through by whoever was acting as duty officer for the day and the backup duty officer took calls if it was necessary to investigate immediately, or they appeared in a worker's in-tray as if by magic. It wasn't like that in other teams, Jake reflected, where they held allocation meetings and chatted about how to handle the referrals. In his previous team, all work was brought for discussion so the team knew what was coming in. It gave you an idea of what would be followed up and what would not. It also was a way of knowing what colleagues were dealing with. The variety of work was one of the things which had originally attracted Jake to this type of social work. It always amazed him how many different facets there were to the job and how no two days at work were ever the same.

Social services was set up as one of those organisations which is seen as something different to everyone who comes into contact with them. More recently, there had been a government-led reorganisation, with mainstream Children's Services now aligned to Education Services and Adult and Mental Health Services linked with Health Services. They each have several major responsibilities as social care agencies and they are still often referred to collectively as Social Services. They deal with adults who need support from the welfare state including those who are mentally ill or disabled, alongside the health and medical services. However, the part that seems to hit the headlines most often is the children's section. Apart from supporting children in need and children with disabilities, children's services are also the providers of care for children who cannot live at home. With the Police, they are one of the two lead agencies charged with the responsibility of keeping children safe from abuse and investigating child abuse. It is here, as bottom-and-bruise inspectors and parent-teller-offers, as Jake had heard one child explain to another, that the upsets are caused both to parents and to society. The problem is that when they get it right, nobody knows and when they don't, everybody knows and knows how to do it better.

In this team, he suspected that the team manager, Frances Phillips, was a bully. She didn't like it to be known she overloaded some and protected others. The secret allocation of work enabled her greater control. Over workloads, over type of work, over pressure of work, over who was the duty worker and how often. Even over mileage expenses. Your staff never knew what work others were doing if work allocation wasn't open.

Jake glanced quickly at his new referrals. Matthew Longstaff, fourteen years old with Myotonic Dystrophy whose family needed some form of support or respite care. He'd have to find out about Myotonic Dystrophy. Interestingly, a transfer from Sally. He wondered what that was about.

Another child with an unspecified disability, Harley Moss. Five months, some sort of seizures. Referral from the GP. Young single mum coping bravely but needing support. Daley Stevens, fifteen. Out of control. Mother wants him in care to teach him a lesson. Jake hated it when parents wanted to get rid of their children. If you didn't want the prize you shouldn't have entered the raffle. However much fun the raffle was fifteen-plus years ago. He's not going to be a popular referral, Jake thought. Teenagers rarely are.

'Anybody seen Monica today?' Tom asked as he entered the room, 'It's just I've got a few visits to do and I'm not going until she's safely off the road and in the office.' He laughed, knowing that Monica, Monnie as she was known, was following him in. Jake glanced up from his letter writing to greet Monica O'Leary who looked for all the world like Merryweather, one of the loveable fairies out of Disney's Sleeping Beauty. Fifty-three, mother of three and from Ireland, Monnie's kindly and matronly looks belied her quick tongue and wicked sense of humour. Her sharp wit and quick reactions were not reflected in her driving and she had recently written off her lease-hire car.

'Fuck me slowly with the ragman's trumpet,' she began, pointing two fingers in a V-shape towards Tom, 'Who let that foulmouthed cunt into this haven of peace and tranquillity? He'll lower the tone so he will.'

Tom smiled. 'Are you putting the kettle on or am I?' A chorus of, Yes pleases followed him out.

Monica continued, 'Now then Jake, how did you get on with Big Roy? Did he give you his What the fuck speech? You didn't let him get away with it did you? And...' the smile left her face, 'which child was it - no injuries please God?'

Jake briefly recounted his visit to the Hegarty household. Monica nodded as he told of the wiping away of the bruise and she briefly brushed the corner of her eye.

'It's not a place for such beautiful babies to be growing up. Research tells us that closure is the precursor to serious damage', she added, slipping into jargon. Jake knew she was alluding to the government research publication, Beyond Blame, and that when families refuse to permit entry to professional agencies, it is social workers that have to recognise the warning signs of potential risk to the children.

And be the poor sods that put their foot in the door.

That afternoon, in the team room, Jake and Lakshmi sat at their desks, almost facing each other on opposite sides of the office.

'Can I ask you a question, Lakshmi?' Jake began.

'Sure,' with a quick smile. Lakshmi was a committed Hindu woman of 42. She was divorced with a son of 14 and as a divorced Hindu woman did not enjoy the unconditional support of her four brothers or her oldest sister, all of whom shared the view that a good woman should be married with a husband. She did, however, enjoy the unconditional support of Puja, her younger sister by two years who was also divorced. A petite, elegant woman who usually favoured a sari or occasionally salwar kameez, today Lakshmi was wearing joggers and a sweat shirt. She smiled, straight teeth and high cheekbones evident, looking expectantly at Jake.

'You don't appear to say much. You don't feel left out, do you?'

'Not at all, it's just in my culture, we women don't tend to start conversations often and sometimes I don't fully understand the slang everyone uses.'

Jake looked first surprised, then quizzical. 'English isn't your first language, then?'

'Gujerati. In fact I think in Gujerati and translate it to speak. I'm not from here. My family had to leave Uganda in 1972 and arrived in the UK with nothing. Really we've done very well, especially when you realise my mother was widowed very young and had seven children to bring up on her own.' Jake pondered this for a while. Lakshmi was always working quietly, never complained and had her files more up to date than anyone else in the team. An ideal employee and Jake had the impression she was popular with the children with whom she worked. He was surprised to learn that he and Lakshmi lived two roads away from each other and Jake suggested she pop in if she was passing and to bring partner, son or anyone else. He was interested to learn more about her culture.

Lakshmi was pleased with the conversation. 'Thanks, Jake. I may well do that some time.' They returned to their files.

Another day on duty. That entails being the one who deals with any new or unallocated people who visit, telephone or write in and put it down as a referral. The problem, thought Jake, is that referral forms don't really do what they are meant to. What they are there for is to be the first record of information to the department which will point the way to what needs to be done. It would be better if you could read a referral and know what the person giving you the information intended with it. Instead what you more often than not get is a form detailing the name and age of the Child, the Doctor, Teacher, Parents, Ethnic Origin in approved format, Health Visitor, School Nurse and Siblings. You have a record of What The Problem Is, but then it takes some digging to find out What Is Required. The problem people tell to children's services is not necessarily the problem that needs to be dealt with.

Sue walked over from her reception desk to interrupt his train of thought,

'I've two people waiting here to see you in reception: Mr Wheeler, who we don't know, who wants to speak about his grand-daughter and Curtis Wilson, who's seriously out of breath. Have a word with me before you see Curtis and I'll give you some background.'

'I'm Jake Atkinson, duty officer for today, Mr Wheeler. How can I help?' Before Jake sat a slim elderly man, possibly late sixties, his white hair meticulously greased into a side-parting to unsuccessfully hide a bald head. Pedal-bin hairstyle when the wind blows, Jake observed to himself. He had a pencil thin moustache covering the lower half of his stiff upper lip and a regimental tie in a Windsor knot round a frayed shirt collar.

Clarence Wheeler leaned forward and placing his palms on his cavalry twills, began, 'I'm a Magistrate.' Jake nodded, to prompt him to continue, but he seemed to have stopped.

Jake thought he detected a slight wobble of his lower lip, before he continued, 'It's my grand-daughter, Emily. She's been to see her father this weekend just gone and her mother doesn't think it's all in order.' Anticipating another long pause, Jake started taking a few notes.

'Are you her maternal Grandfather?'

'I am that and my daughter is a single parent and a damn good one at that,' he said firmly.

Jake wrote down Possible Sexual Abuse, in anticipation of the allegation to come, then asked ' A n d how old is Emily?'

'Thirty-five months. That's three shortly.' In an Announcement tone. Jake realised that this was a difficult task for the man opposite and decided to prompt him.

'What is it that you've actually come to tell me, Mr Wheeler?' he asked in a lowered voice.

'Sandra – that's my daughter, says when Emily stayed with her father last weekend...' he briefly paused then whispered, 'he touched her Virginia.' He stopped and his tight lips went tighter as he sucked on his moustache.

During the two or three minute silence that followed, Jake suppressed a smile. Virginia was a new word to him when talking about female genitalia. He'd heard various other names - fi-fi, fou-fou, fanny, foof, fuffy, flower, flue, front bottom, flange, bits, mou-mou, mary, minney, mimi, muff, ha'penny, tuppence, spot, growler, dinky, binky, minky, pinky, minge, grumble, nunny, nonny, cherry, punanee, privates, wanny, toybox, tanunu, whatsit, down there, down below, downstairs and various others. But never Virginia. Magistrate speak. Virginia Creeper Your Worship, he thought.

'What's the form then, what happens next?' Mr Wheeler rose as if to go. Jake gestured for him to sit back down and explained that he would need more information first. Showing him the form, he painstakingly ran through all the names, addresses and other areas needed. Twenty minutes later, having advised him that Sandra, the child's mother would need to seek legal advice over contact arrangements, he ushered the elderly man out. Mr Wheeler departed in crisp military style, his upper lip still stiff and his lower lip decidedly wobbly.

Conscious that Mr Wheeler had been one of two people waiting to see him, Jake looked in on Sue for information about Curtis Wilson, the other one.

'Curtis is sixteen but it's not Curtis you need to know about; it's his mother Dolly. She's not the full Shilling.' Tapping the side of her head.

'Diagnosed?'

'I'm not sure, but I'd imagine so - up and down like a yo-yo. The higher she gets, the stronger the Patois. And poor Curtis has to translate. Last time she was here it was to say Tom Davey was turning her boy into a Battyman - whatever that is.'

'Homosexual. She's Jamaican, then?' he intervened.

'That's right and Curtis normally comes in when she's up in the...' Sue went silent, having taken in Jake's explanation, then added with an embarrassed smile, 'Are you sure that's what it means? I told her I thought Curtis'd make an excellent cricketer at the time.' Jake thought it best to leave her to work out her feelings and made his way through to see Curtis in the interview room.

Jake looked across the interview room at the young man opposite. Skinny five-feet ten, a handsome black youth in a school uniform slightly too short. Beads of sweat on his forehead. Possibly nerves, maybe heat.

'It's my Mum,' he began, 'have they told you about her?'

Jake nodded, 'Some.'

'She's locked the Gas Man in the cellar this morning and won't let him out until the meter reading's lower. I didn't know where else to go and I don't want her to be put away.'

'How ill is she at the moment? Do I call the Doctor?' asked Jake.

Curtis wrinkled his nose before replying slowly, 'Not too bad at the moment, like she's not seeing or hearing things that aren't there, nor nothing. She's just locked the Gas Man in the cellar, that's all. If someone in authority tells her, she'll let him go.' For a minute he had an imploring look of desperation in his big brown eyes.

'Are you okay yourself?' asked Jake. He felt very sad for this sixteen year old who had to make adult decisions; 'What if I can get a police officer to pop round informally?'

'As long as she won't be arrested, I don't care who does it,' Curtis responded.

'Bear with me, Sir,' the voice on the other end of the line said, then 'Police control.' Brusquely. Jake explained his position and that Dolly Wilson had a stuck cellar door, with a Gas Man on the wrong side of it who was being blamed for the size of the debt. The police officer's tone changed, as he burst into laughter.

'We know Dolly. I'll get one of the lads round ten-four. Leave it with me.' Jake told Curtis that it should be sorted out quickly and he should go off to school.

Before he departed, Jake asked casually, as an afterthought, what was Curtis' favourite sport and was encouraged when cricket came back as the answer.

Two days later, it was Friday and a reasonable spring morning in March. Jake had found time between the paperwork and the office duty to start on some of his new visits. He turned his Peugeot 407 into Fairways Close, hoping that the letter he had sent to Sarah Moss yesterday had arrived this morning. There was a brass doorbell and a brass lion's head knocker on the blue painted door to number 17. Jake paused briefly before choosing the doorbell. A pleasant and pretty young woman answered and smiling enquired, 'Is it Mr Atkinson?'

'Please call me Jake,' he responded as he walked in. 'You must be Sarah Moss and I assume this is Harley.'

He looked at the baby, who was sitting on the deep green carpet playing with an Activity Centre. He was dressed in a tiny pair of denim dungarees with corduroy slippers. His blond hair fell over his ears in soft ringlets, framing quite the prettiest baby face Jake thought he had ever seen. A pair of deep blue eyes like saucers looked back at him as Harley's mouth widened into a smile to show just two bottom teeth. Framing his mouth was the remains of half a Bickiepeg, the other half of which was attached to a ribbon around his neck.

Jake resisted the overwhelming desire to pick him up, as Sarah interrupted. 'Would you like tea or coffee?'

'Coffee, black no sugar, if it's no trouble please,' he responded, noting with some relief the cleanliness of the room.

Sarah moved next door into the kitchen, turning on the kettle and then quietly moved through to the mirror in the downstairs toilet. There she checked her makeup in the mirror, pulled her short skirt a little higher on her waist and adjusted the buttons on the front of her blouse so that the top of her bra could just be seen. Quite nice, she thought to herself about Jake, but a bit old to be really fanciable. Still, no harm in seeing where you stand. You never know when you might need a friend in the right place.

As she came back in carrying a steaming cup, Jake was sitting on the floor with Harley, his hand playing spiders over the Activity Centre while the child gave a deep gurgling laugh. He looked up and thanked Sarah for the coffee, returning to the dralon armchair. As Sarah sat opposite, he wondered how so young a mother could cope with all the stress Harley's condition must bring. She had the same deep blue eyes as Harley and her shoulder length hair had a just-brushed look about it.

'I've come to see what help we can offer you to cope with the difficulties in caring for your son. I'm aware he has had some medical problems and I'm sure it must be very difficult for you.'

Sarah's eyes filled with tears, 'I'm always afraid that he'll go the same way as Liam.'

'Liam?'

'His older brother - it was eighteen months ago. He died in his sleep. Cot death, they called it. He was only three months old. That's him.' She pointed to a picture in a frame on top of the television, showing a small bald baby apparently asleep in a carrycot. Jake had seen it, but had assumed it was a picture of Harley.

'What about your family - is there anyone to support you and help you out?'

'They're all down in Spalding in Lincolnshire - I don't really see them,' she sniffed. Jake felt it might upset her to pursue this line of questions further. Another time. He turned back to Harley and smiled. 'You've a son to be proud of there - he's lovely.' Sarah shot a smile very similar to Harley's in return.

A little girl really, he thought. And Harley's like a china doll. The tears had gone as quickly as they had come, he noticed. After a half-hour spent discussing the problems and pressures Sarah had in coping with Harley, Jake had come to the conclusion that she was socially isolated.

'Shall I come and see you in a couple of weeks to see how things are going and what the doctors are going to do about tests? I can chase them up if you like. Perhaps you'd like me to see if I can arrange a place at a mother and toddler group. Will a visit in a fortnight be okay?'

Noting Sarah's agreement, he put a reminder in his diary and giving an extra wave to the baby, he left.

Daley was sitting in an armchair when Jake arrived. Right in an armchair. He couldn't have curled into a smaller space in the chair even if he had wanted to. Angela Stevens was going to let this social worker know exactly what the score was. She wanted something done before she went into the maternity wing at the hospital. Preferably Daley removed.

''E's a little bastard,' she began. 'The little fucker drinks and takes drugs, stays out till all hours of the day and night. 'E's been stealing, 'e's violent…' she paused for breath, her deep red lipstick round a downturned mouth contorted with hate. Barely stopping, she continued. 'And 'is fuckin' language, well, I don't know where 'e gets it from.'

Jake had an idea where, but thought he would save that discussion for another time. Before he could say anything, she was away again. 'Sex, the little bastard's been having sex with some slapper on my fucking sofa while I was at Megasave's and he's nicked a fiver out of my purse to buy fags and…' She paused for effect and her brown eyes narrowed to slits. ''E's been wagging it.'

Jake suddenly had great difficulty suppressing the urge to laugh. He wanted to ask who the boy had been wagging it at and why this was so much more serious than all his other misdemeanours. Keeping a straight face he looked for the first time at Daley, who was still curled up in the armchair. He was a good looking boy, tall and gangly, even featured, quite muscular, with skin the colour of coffee with cream and a plaited Dame Kelly Holmes cane-row hairstyle topped with a Nike IQ reducer cap. His green eyes had long dark lashes and were filled with tears which ran silently down his face and dripped off his chin onto a red polo shirt. His shoulders shook as he cried without a sound.

Angela must have recognised Jake's blank expression and she shouted, 'Wagging, you know, wagging school,' and added venomously, 'the little shit.'

'What's Daley's view on all this – what does he want?' Jake began and was interrupted before he could continue with, 'A bloody good hiding so's 'e bleeds – that's what 'e bloody well wants and that's what 'e'll get if you don't take 'im and put 'im somewhere 'cause I'll fucking kill the foulmouthed little brat if'n you don't.'

Jake was aware he was going to have to find somewhere for the lad. He couldn't leave him at home.

'Have you anything you'd want to say to your son if I was going to take him away?' Jake asked. Angela turned to look at Daley, his shoulders still shaking and tears still running down his face. Jake thought her face had softened a little until she spoke.

'I still want my fiver back. Remove the little bastard now.'

'I'm not taking him now, because I've to talk to my boss first. I also want to spend some time talking to him alone.'

'You're not shifting me out of my own lounge. Take 'im somewhere else to talk.' No point in arguing. It's like disposing of an unwanted pet, Jake thought to himself. Why do they have them in the first place? Her pregnancy was obviously well advanced. How long before we're back to remove the next one? Poor little soul. Jake looked at Daley's IQ reducer, a baseball cap put on backwards, now slipped to one side. It had worked its way loose on the back of the chair and sat on Daley's head like a beret, as Daley's sobbing, still silent, continued.

Jake had never seen such a clean car as Sally Beckett's Ford Ka. It was a sort of silver-and–lavender colour, with a little space on the front dashboard for floral tissues. He had secretly wondered if he should have taken his shoes off before accepting a lift from her. As they pulled into Elizabeth Road, Sally pulled up outside a house with a vastly overgrown privet hedge.

'This is where Matthew and his family live. He's a nice lad …really.' She didn't sound convinced.

'We're round back – nowt posh 'ere.' The voice belonged to a weathered man in his fifties, who came from a path along the side of the house. He was smoking a roll-up which stayed in his mouth and waggled up and down as he spoke. He wore a vest, baggy flannel trousers and tartan slippers with holes in both big toes. A long dirty toenail poked through on each foot, which struck Jake as strange, as he was wearing socks into which his trousers were tucked. His bottle-bottom glasses were held together on one side by a pink sticking plaster. As he held out a grubby hand to shake with Jake, Jake noticed a bare-breasted mermaid tattooed on his forearm.

'Victor Longstaff – I'm Matthew's Dad. You must be that Mester Atkins Sally told us about, come to do for our Matthew and that. Eh up Sally, come on in.'

'Jacob Atkinson, Mr Longstaff. Please call me Jake.'

As Jake and Sally went through the kitchen into the lounge, Jake found himself reminded of Albert Steggles and wondered if he was any nearer to getting a job.

'And this is our Matthew.' He raised his voice to a shout in the direction of the boy waiting in his wheelchair. 'Say hello to the Mester, he's your new social worker.'

Jake turned to smile at Matthew, whose speech was clearly limited by his disability, but he managed an indistinct nasal 'Hello.' Matthew's Myotonic Dystrophy affected his ability to do most things. He had very limited use of his arms, was unable to walk and had severe speech and learning disabilities. His appearance also reflected his father's lack of concern for hygiene. He was similarly poor-sighted and like his father, had his glasses repaired with a pink sticking plaster that looked as if it may have been recycled. His chin and upper lip were covered in bumfluff. Black teeth and brown curly breath, Jake thought, as he perched as near the edge of the sofa as he reasonably could, with Sally similarly perched on his left.

'I was really only wanting to meet you today and make an appointment to…' Jake began, but Vic Longstaff was having none of it.

'Lovely girl, our Sally.' He was straining to look beyond her raised knees in an attempt to see up her skirt. 'If I were twenty years younger...' And he winked suggestively, slipping his hands into his pockets. 'Tell the mester what you've been doing today, Matthew,' he shouted at his son, 'Tell 'im, go on tell 'im. At school. Wi' Miss 'awkins.'

Matthew smiled, dribbling as he did so, ''oo'in.' With a sinking feeling, Jake had the distinct impression it might be Cooking Matthew was saying. Before he could check, Matthew's father had left the room and returned with a grubby biscuit tin.

'Cheese straws, delicious, Matthew.' Jake said, as he opened the tin and finding a collection of what looked like greyish greasy sticks, 'Did you make them all yourself?' Matthew nodded enthusiastically. 'I wish I could try one, but I've got an allergy to cheese,' Jake continued.

He hoped this would be the end of the demonstration, but Vic was determined.

'She'll 'ave one, won't you Sally. They're lovely – we've et loads. You'd not disappoint the lad would you?'

Sally scanned the contents of the tin and carefully picked out a small one. Three sets of eyes watched her hand as it moved towards her handbag, then, as she noticed she was being watched, it changed its path to move towards her mouth. She ate slowly, forcing a smile as she did so, while Jake made a next appointment to visit.

As they drove back in Sally's Ford Ka, she turned briefly towards Jake. 'What did you think?'

'I couldn't decide whether I was more put off those cheese straws by their colour, the spit and dribble or by those filthy fingernails'

Sally refused to speak to him for the rest of that day.

# Three

The office suddenly became quiet as Jake walked in. It was a quarter to two.

He greeted Monica in passing, 'Everything alright?'

'Keep your fucking head down – the Ayatollah's a bit arsey. Like a Bull with a headache. She's after your bollocks...' Her voice had dropped to a whisper.

Chrissie came out of Frances, the team manager's office, carrying a cup to the kitchen. 'Frances wants to start your supervision early, like now.' Jake was sure she was smirking.

'I realise you haven't been with us for very long and you're not fully conversational with the way things are done here,' Frances began. Jake wondered what was coming next and was he to be treated to more of Frances's malapropisms. 'At the end of the day, come the Inquiry, I have to be answerable for all your work. So whatever the benefits or disbenefits of your particular casework methods, I need to be kept appraised. Do I make myself clear?'

Absolutely not, Jake thought. He nodded nevertheless. 'Is there something in particular with which you're concerned?' he asked, wondering what on earth she was talking about.

'You were the last social worker to visit the Hegarty family. That was two weeks ago. Now one of the twins is dead. What I want to know is what sort of risk assessment you carried out and if our department is going to get any blame. I've had Christine as an experienced worker audit your case notes and I am not aware from your initial assessment that you did anything to check on the welfare of those twins.'

Jake was not concentrating. He could only think of a small pair of brown eyes peering at him through a letterbox.

'Was it Ricky or Ryan?' He couldn't remember much about Ryan.

'I don't remember which one, but it's a mute point. Fortunately we're not in the firing line here yet, but the fact remains I'm not happy about your lack of risk assessment.' Jake suppressed an urge to reply, either in defence of his actions or criticism at the lack of explanation. He decided to make it a mute point and keep quiet.

'What else have you got? I've recently passed you three more. Have you undertaken an initial assessment yet on them?'

Jake detailed his visit to Angela and Daley Stevens. 'I can't see any alternative but to accommodate the lad,' he finished.

While detailing his visit to the Hegarty household he found it hard not to concentrate on the dead twin. How would the other one manage? How had he died? Was it the letterbox boy?

'I know there's a place at Beech Lodge because Sally's just moved one out. Give them a ring about Daley. Alison Bryant's the Officer-in-Charge and she owes me a favour. Tell them I suggested you ring direct and it's a planned emergency.'

Jake was surprised. He had been informed of the difficulty in finding places for children. Usually it went to the Combined Areas Placement Panel, who would tell you there were neither residential nor foster care places available immediately, due to emergency allocations. Certain teams appeared to have more emergencies than others, it seemed to Jake. Certain emergencies and he guessed this included the planned ones, took priorities for reasons he suspected that he was just beginning to find out. He briefly wondered what a planned emergency was and whether Daley fitted the criteria.

'Can I ask what happened to the Hegarty child,' he went on tentatively, 'Only...' he wasn't quite sure what to say, but realised he was feeling profoundly distressed.

'It shouldn't be seen to be our fault and beyond that it doesn't really matter, does it?' chirped Frances, brightly. 'Now, what about our baby with the blue fits?'

Jake felt a little embarrassed at the thought of telling Frances he suspected that Sarah, the child's mother might be flirting with him. He thought it wise to mention it at a later date if it became any more blatant. Instead, he kept the conversation centred on Harley. Jake watched Frances making notes in her large leaning writing. He was curious to see if her writing reflected the poor standard of English in her speech. As he repeated and explained the meaning of Cyanotic Episodes, he was quietly amused to see upside-down that she had written what looked like Boy has Blue Tits.

'Finally, I've had a complaint that you've been using bad language in the team room. This isn't good enough. It's got to be deleted forthwith.' Frances looked at him over her glasses.

'Chrissie McBride?' Jake thought he knew the answer.

'Christine, Tom, Monica and Sally have all confirmed that your language is, on occasion, unacceptable.'

As Jake walked back into the team room, the other five members of the team stopped talking.

'Good supervision?' Tom asked.

Jake was still thinking about the toddler that had died. 'One of the Hegarty twins,' he began, but was interrupted.

'Ricky. Pushed out of the bedroom window by the other. Subdural Haematoma. DOA as they say in America,' interrupted Tom. 'We know. And?'

'My language in the office is inappropriate.' Explosions of laughter erupted from Monnie and Tom, with smiles from Sally, Chrissie and Lakshmi, the sixth social worker.

'Fucking foul-mouthed bastard. Don't do it again,' Monnie giggled.

Jake smiled, but could still see in his mind two little brown eyes peeping through a letterbox and as he left he felt a lump forming in his throat.

Two-and-a-half days per week on duty. At least. A significant amount of time dealing with the unexpected while you've still got a caseload. Still, Jake mused, it's better to be a stand-in social worker than to be tied to one team forever. Every Christmas or school summer holidays, 'I've lost my purse in the park and the ninety-seven pounds I had in it for the kids' treats is all gone...' It's one of the great mysteries in social work how families surviving on under fifty pounds a week always lose their purses in the park and it's always had just under one hundred pounds in at the time.

As a supply, agency or locum social worker as stand-ins are sometimes called, Jake could work for as long as he wished within a team then opt to move on. Because his role was to fill in for long term sickness, unfilled vacancies and to cover areas of need, he could choose virtually any team he wanted. The Council's intended thirteen percent vacancy rate was running at over twenty-five percent among qualified social workers and the cracks, he thought, were beginning to show.

Jake was driving home and his thoughts turned to Daley. Regret, really. Angela had wanted to manipulate Social Services to remove him and he'd done just that.

The Peugeot joggled over the cat's-eyes as he turned right onto St Andrew's Road. It was almost seven o'clock as he approached his driveway on Thorncliffe Road. As he walked up the stairs to the front door of his flat, he had a mental image of two eyes and a letterbox. Ricky again – or was it Ryan? Either way, he thought, he won't get any more battle scars from his brother. The lump returned to his throat.

Jake's flat was on the first and second floor of an Edwardian house in Mapperley Park. His thirty-foot lounge must have been a very impressive master bedroom some ninety years prior. Now it made a great room for a stereo fan. Jake selected the Schindler's List Theme from a wall-mounted rack of CDs as he changed into Reebok lycras and donned a well-worn pair of Asics Kayanos for his evening run. He briefly tilted his left foot as he tied the laces, with memories of a split-front smile in Albert's shoes.

Jake relaxed into the run, padding the frustrations of the day into the pavement as he went. A gentle rain started to fall as he crossed the Park and Ride towards the Arboretum and it cooled him as he sweated lightly and accelerated up the hill. Questions began to fill his mind as the rain dissipated. The grass below his feet across the Arboretum gave slight spring to his pace. Another hill. What message do they give, he wondered. Sarah Moss with her slightly too open buttons and Sally Beckett with her slightly too closed lips, with just the right amount of gloss. His thoughts moved on to Lakshmi. It can't be easy being a Hindu woman in a white organisation. Nice woman and so together. She obviously has her life well organised.

Short dip, short climb. He thought he could read Sally, with her appearance perfected to mask her insecurity, but not Sarah. Her whole life revolves around Harley. Doesn't it? So why did she never look tired after a sleepless night and where's the baby dribble on her clothing? Is she flirting? If so, why with someone whose age and position prevents the possibility of any personal interaction? And how on earth does she always find the time to make herself up so carefully? And why? Mortician style. Not so much slap as slab.

Three miles and twenty five minutes later, Jake was approaching home again and his thoughts had once again changed. He was humming 'Sultans of Swing' to himself in time to his footfalls and thinking about eating. He'd been catering for himself since Geraldine, his partner, had left him some six weeks previously. They'd been together for three years. Jake had thought it was an easygoing and close partnership, but passionless. Geraldine, in her slim, willowy way seemed to drift from one shopping trip to the next. When she'd announced she was leaving him for a real lover, he'd been quietly disappointed but not surprised. When she told him her new lover's name was Sylvia, Jake began to question his own adequacy. He hadn't imagined. His first thoughts were that she might shave off her beautiful brown hair, put on three stone and grow a moustache. Lesbian colleagues he'd worked with always seemed to have short greased back hair and huge pendulous breasts under a political T-shirt. Geraldine was slim and almost hippy-like with a dreamy approach to life. And now she was living somewhere else.

Home after a decent run. Pleasant warm light-headedness. Jake put Ma Vlast on the stereo and decided on grilled cod with rice and mixed beans, followed by two cans of Stella, then settled down to watch a repeat of 'House' on Freeview. Later in bed, just as he was drifting off to sleep, he remembered, '…And tell your boss, Frances Fucking Phillips…'

Charmectomy, the pair of them, he thought.

It was a hot Wednesday in May. Sarah Moss was wheeling Harley in his McLaren baby buggy up to the doors of her local Megasave supermarket. Harley was looking particularly sweet that day in his white and blue striped Osh Kosh dungarees which fitted him just perfectly. He had blue corduroy playboots on his feet, on which were pictures of teddies. His blond curls had a just-washed look and Sarah rightly knew that passers-by would smile at him and make gurgly noises, laughing as he smiled back at them. The weather forecast had predicted twenty four degrees and it felt as if it was at least that.

As Sarah and Harley approached the doors of Megasave there was an elderly woman on a motorised invalid scooter, blocking the doorway. A Saga lout on a meep-meep. Sarah waited patiently. Harley, with beads of sweat on his top lip, began to arch his back in the buggy. As the woman was not moving, Sarah said, timidly, 'Can I pass, please?' The elderly woman turned in her buggy to look at Sarah. Her tortoise-like face was contorted with a look of anger.

'I'm eighty-three, me.' And she scowled at Sarah. The scooter remained motionless in the doorway. Sarah looked embarrassed and said nothing.

She turned Harley's buggy and headed for the trolley park. She stopped by the metal snake of supermarket trolleys and finding her purse, took a pound coin from it, placing it into the coin slot on the trolley. Having pulled the trolley loose from the snake with some effort, she bent to unstrap Harley from his buggy. She held Harley on her hip with her left arm and deftly folded the buggy with her right hand, sliding it under the basket on the base of the trolley. She swung Harley up into the air with both hands under his arms,

'Wheeeee!' Harley giggled. A long throaty giggle. As she lowered him towards the trolley seat, Harley straightened his legs and arched his back, apparently unwilling to be sat in the trolley. Sarah patiently fed his legs one at a time into the holes at the front of the seat.

'You little monkey,' smiling and touching nose-to-nose as she did so. Once in, Harley sat motionlessly and Sarah once more approached the entrance door. As she got to the door she watched the invalid scooter, with several people waiting behind it, kangaroo through the open door in short, sharp jerks. An eighty-three year old head jerked back and forth like a rodeo cowboy's on a bucking bronco. As Sarah pushed the shopping trolley through the now clear front door of Megasave, she slowed as she felt the cooling blast from above of the air conditioning. Inside, she stopped and sniffed, noticing the smell of baking bread. She turned left, then right towards the cosmetics and pharmacy section.

As she approached the shampoos, she saw three black youths gathered at the shampoo shelf. All three had a gangly look, as if controlled by an inattentive puppeteer.

The tallest of them, some five foot ten, was holding a bottle of shampoo up in front of the other two.

'This fo' Rebellious Hair.' An assumed and exaggerated southern black American accent. He had two-inch locks and denims so loose from the waist downwards, they looked almost like a skirt. 'Re-bellious hair! Looky looky here, I'm Re-bellious hair. I'm gwine up, git on my Hog an' high-tail it outta here. Then you be Bald. Yo' head like an ol' chocolate egg. Huh. Then you be sorry. Mmmm, Mmmm, Mmmm.' In descending tones.

The other two youths erupted into cackling laughter, one of them whooping as he did so. Sarah tutted and, as she wheeled the trolley round them, gave a wry smile to herself as she thought of Dumbo's crows. She watched as two security men approached.

She wanted a bottle of shampoo, but decided to reject the Shampoo for Rebellious Hair. Quickly picking shampoo for dry, damaged or coloured hair and conditioner to match, she moved to the next aisle to closely examine the tablet and medicine section.

As she approached the bakery, a kindly looking woman leaning on her shopping trolley smiled as they passed. 'Aaaah.'

Sarah smiled a proud acknowledgement and, shoulders back, walked on to continue with her shopping. Twenty minutes later, with a half-full shopping trolley

Sarah approached the checkout counters. There were queues at all of them.

She joined one to watch the Asian shop assistant, her name badge reading Bhalwant, announce into a tannoy by her till, in slow, crisp, clear tones, 'Supervisor, Kotex double absorbent panty liners, thirty-six box. Price please.'

Across the counter, a woman in her thirties with a red face was shifting from one foot to another and whispering loudly and desperately, 'Put them back. I don't want them, I don't want them.'

Sarah shifted direction and moved purposefully with her trolley towards the restaurant area. Stopping and lifting Harley out, she parked the trolley in one of the trolley lockers. She walked into the ladies' toilet with Harley on her hip.

Shoppers paused five minutes later, as the loudspeakers announced loudly, 'First Aid, restaurant area, urgently. First Aid, restaurant area, urgently.' The store first aider, Janet Miller, approached to observe a ring of shoppers gathered round a neat, well-dressed young woman in a short skirt, holding a limp baby, almost blue in colour. The young woman appeared beside herself, her face red with tears,

'He's had another fit, he's had another fit.' She repeated it over and over, sobbing uncontrollably as she did so. Janet, an assistant manager, wise, experienced and motherly, calmly sat Sarah on a soft seat.

Checking Harley's pulse and gently looking in his mouth, she said, 'He's got a strong regular heartbeat and he's breathing fine. The ambulance will be along in a minute.' She looked at Harley. 'His colour's improving rapidly. I'm sure he'll be fine.' She had a soothing, kindly voice and Sarah's crying lessened. The customers dispersed, in a sombre mood muttering sympathetically to each other.

As Janet passed the customer services desk, the customer services manager, Barry, touched her arm. 'I saw her go in seconds before and the baby looked fine. It must have come on lightning-quick.'

Janet responded. 'Yes, strange; I've never seen anything like it. Poor girl, she can't be more than a teenager herself.' She walked back to her office, deep in thought.

At the back of the shop, in the staff car park, in a covered enclave where Megasave employees normally gathered to smoke, there was also a small cluster of people. Several white men, two of them in uniform were stood encircling a black teenager, originally one of three. The other two had successfully run away.

Sarah's shopping was packed for her by the store manager, Mike Larkin, who was in attendance. 'Don't worry about it; you can settle with us next time or whatever.'

In the smoker's cave, as it was known, Curtis Wilson was being held by two of the men, as a third man, one of those in uniform, repeatedly hit the teenager several times in the stomach area.

Sarah and Harley were bundled into an ambulance. Sarah's face was still red from crying. Harley, colour returned, was trying to reach the packet of Jaffa Cakes in Sarah's shopping bag.

The ambulance sped off, its siren wailing. Another siren, as if in answer to the first, could be heard approaching.

During the following week Jake would spend much of his waking time thinking about Ricky Hegarty. He'd spent the week catching up on recording his visits and preparing the paperwork to arrange for Daley Stevens to be taken to Beech Lodge, where, as Frances had correctly predicted, he had been found a bed. Beech Lodge was a grand Edwardian mansion with two entrances to the driveway. There may have been beech trees at one time but now it was fronted with a scraggy conifer hedge some fifteen feet high. The front entrance of panelled oak double doors was framed by a pillared stone arch. Written diagonally in lipstick across the left door was the word, 'Wank' and across the right, 'Jacko Raz'.

Jake stood in front of the doors looking for a bell to ring. There was no door bell and as he pondered what to do a familiar voice whispered in his ear.

'It's an initiative test for thick social workers.' He turned round to see Monnie grinning. She reached past him and pushed the door open adding quietly, 'As much use as a chocolate dildo. You just can't get the staff these days.'

'Oh, hi Monnie,' Jake responded, 'what are you doing here?'

'Same as you, come to see a child, but while I'm here I wanted a word with you. What I need to tell you is about that Frances Phillips. Watch her, do not trust her with anything and do not give her any information you do not have to.' Monnie continued to Jake, 'That woman will twist it and use it. She'll tell lies; she'll do anything to protect her own back. She's not good, she's not nice and she's not honest. Don't trust her. You take the word of one older and wiser than you.'

Jake was a bit curious about this information but said nothing. He was also uncomfortable about walking in to Beech Lodge without knocking or being invited. It was, after all, someone's home. And soon to be Daley's. There was something not right about everyone just being able to march in. He could see no alternative though and he followed Monnie through a large entrance hall to a closed door at the far end.

Monnie walked through the large oak-panelled hallway with Jake and knocked on a door labelled Office. It opened to reveal four adults sitting drinking coffee. Jake could hear children shouting and running upstairs. He wondered how many staff were in the building.

Monnie looked across the room at a slim blonde woman in her late twenties. 'Ah, Alison nice to see you. I believe this young man wants a word with you. Alison Bryant meet Jake Atkinson.'

The slim blonde woman stood up and smiled. She was even-featured with straight teeth, shoulder length blond hair with a centre parting and wearing a black T-shirt and denim jeans.

'Alison's the officer in charge here,' Monnie went on, 'the Boss. She makes all the decisions. She decides...' she went on with a twinkle in her eye, '...whether or not you get a cup of coffee when you ask for one.' And she giggled, again.

Alison Bryant stood up and turned towards Jake, 'You've come to speak about a young man you want a bed for here? Have you brought me any paperwork?' Jake nodded bringing out of his bag several coloured forms.

'Here they are - LAC forms.'

Looked After Children forms, known as LAC forms, are the standard forms needing to be filled in up and down the United Kingdom whenever a child is to be placed in any sort of accommodation by Children's Services; they were designed as an attempt to standardise information. Like many social workers Jake found them intensely frustrating to fill in as so much information had to be repeated on each form.

Alison quickly glanced through them and said, 'Yes these seem fine. He's what - fifteen? He's of mixed ethnic origin. What's he like?'

Jake looked up and said, 'Yes fifteen. He seems to be a pleasant young man; he doesn't say very much to me but he's…'

'No, no,' Alison said. 'Is he mature, is he immature, does he eat much, is he bright?'

'He seems fairly mature,' said Jake, 'I'm not sure how bright he is and I have no idea to what extent he eats; but he's a teenager so you can expect a good appetite.'

'Three 'D's?'

'I'm sorry?' Jake looked at Alison. Attractive blue eyes.

'Disturbed, Delinquent or Drug user?'

'Not as far as I know, although, if you were to take the word of his mother, and I'm not sure I would, he's the Devil incarnate. But he seems like a fairly normal 15-year old to me. Well-named – he's got the good looks of a young Daley Thompson'

'That's fair enough,' said Alison. 'I'll see you on Monday with him. Have you any questions?'

'Just a couple,' responded Jake. 'How many staff do you have here and how many residents?'

'Just got four staff on duty at any one time,' said Alison. 'We were in the office when you came. There are eleven youngsters at the moment, four girls and seven boys. Daley will be our twelfth child and that makes up our quota. Occasionally the Emergency Duty Team tries to palm a child off on us at night but we usually manage to resist them. Daley will have his own room, with a lock on the door and he'll be able to decorate it as he wants. I'm sure he'll be very happy here. If he's not, I'll see to him myself.'

Jake was not quite sure what she meant by that but let the remark go. 'See you Monday then.'

As Jake left he wondered how Daley would fit into such a home when he had lived for so long with only his mother. He also wondered what supervision the children received when all of the staff were sitting in the office drinking coffee. He thought that if it affected Daley he may ask questions about that at a later time.

From Beech Lodge he drove to visit Angela and Daley Stevens. He had written to Angela previously saying that he would be coming and that he had a place arranged for Daley in the children's home. As he arrived Angela threw the door open and beamed a welcoming smile.

'Hello young man, how nice to see you. How are you?' Jake was a bit surprised by this because it was so very different from her tone the last time they had met.

'Fine thank you. How's Daley?'

'Oh he's not a bad lad; he's doing fine thanks. He's looking forward to going to the children's home and so…' she smiled, '…am I.'

As Jacob walked into the house he saw Daley sitting in front of a play-station in the lounge. 'Hello Daley,' he started, 'not at school today?'

'Mum said I didn't have to go,' Daley responded, to which Angela nodded. 'She says if I'm not going to be living here much longer then I can do pretty much what I like.'

Jake looked at Angela and said, 'I'm not sure that's ever such a good idea. Nevertheless if you want to spend time with him I can understand that.'

'Oh,' said Angela, 'I don't want to spend time with him, it's just that letting him do whatever he wants stops him from being mardy-arsed.'

Jake decided not to respond. 'Today's Thursday,' he said to Daley, 'I'll come and collect you after school on Monday to take you across to Beech Lodge where you can meet Alison Bryant, the woman in charge. She'll show you where you're going to be sleeping and tell you about the arrangements. I've been there today. It's a posh house. Nothing but the best for you. They've got big wooden doors at the front and a huge hedge and it's ever so grand.'

Daley looked at him, 'I don't care what the building's like. I don't care what any of it's like. I don't really want to go there.' Jake looked at him and felt sad.

'There's nothing I can do about that. Really it's the only place I could get and it was your mother's choice for you to be accommodated by us.' Angela turned sharply and shot a look of pure poison at Jake, but said nothing. Daley shrugged and went back to his play-station.

It was ten o'clock on the following Tuesday and most of the resident children at Beech Lodge were quietly in bed.

The office door opened and Alison Bryant looked up from her paperwork.

Craig Wells hovered. 'It's our new boy, Daley. He's been sobbing in his bedroom for two hours now. I've tried speaking to him, leaving him alone, asking him what I can do, everything. Any ideas?'

Alison put her pen down. 'You and the other staff concentrate on the other kids. I'll see if I can put some of my counselling skills to use to calm him down. Better not to disturb us. I'll call if I need support.'

Ten minutes later, Alison quietly opened the door to Daley's bedroom and tiptoed in, locking the door behind her. The bed shook as the boy quietly sobbed under the quilt. She sat on the edge of the bed and folded back the edge of the quilt cover. Taking his hot head in her arms, she sat him up slightly and cuddled him against her, her chin just above the top of his neatly plaited hair.

'We'll sort it out,' she whispered. 'We'll sort it.'

She stroked the side of his face and, noticing how hot he was, moved the quilt down the bed. As she did so, her hand brushed his stomach over his dark green cotton pyjamas and she noticed how firm and muscular it was.

Daley had stopped sobbing and was laying still, his head against her chest.

'You're hot. Let's cool you down a bit.' She deftly slipped her hand along his buttons and opened his pyjama top. Cradling his head in her left hand, she lightly ran her fingers over his chest and stomach. His bronzed skin was smooth and rippled with muscle. There were beads of sweat down his front. He had that just-washed baby smell and a small dark spot a bit like a bruise below his left nipple. As she explored, she was aware of a pleasurable moist feeling within herself and she slipped Daley's hand between the press studs on the front of her denim blouse. She had no bra and as he began gently rubbing her hardened nipple, she moved down to lightly touch his erection and tilted his head up to kiss his mouth, exploring round his teeth with her tongue.

'Have you done this before?' she whispered. He shook his head and she felt herself become wetter and hotter. She pushed the elastic on Daley's pyjama bottoms down and began to stroke his shaft slowly and watched as a stream of semen spurted up his front as far as his chest. Sitting up, she moved the quilt off the bed completely and removed his pyjamas, bottoms first. As if undressing a baby, she slid his arms out of his pyjama top and, having slid it out from under him, wiped his front with it. As she did so, she noticed his erection beginning to throb back into existence. She pulled his hand from out between the press-studs of her blouse and pulled it open, letting it slip off behind her and fall to the floor. She alternately watched his penis and his eyes as she kicked off her clogs, then slowly unbuttoned her Levi 501's and pulled them down. The damp patch would not show, she hoped, on her black pants. Standing up in front of Daley on the bed, she watched his mesmerised stare as she slowly pulled them down to reveal a tattooed rose overgrown by a light triangular covering of honey-coloured pubic hair. The rose stem disappeared under thicker hair towards her cleft. By now she was so wet with anticipation, she briefly hoped she would not drip on him as she straddled his slim hips and reached behind her to guide him inside. She gasped with pleasure as she felt him enter her, warm and hard. As she moved back and forth on top of him, she saw him watching, apparently unable to look away from the rose moving up and down. After a time, she lowered her body onto him and pulled him to her to rhythmically continue, their stomachs touching and her breasts pressed against his chest. Eventually, she reached a climax as he again ejaculated, this time inside her. She rolled off him and they lay side by side, seemingly exhausted.

'Better now?' she whispered. He nodded, half asleep.

Alison Bryant, Unit Manager, quietly slipped her clothes back on and tiptoed out the door to continue her shift.

It was raining. One of those summery storms where the water bounces off the pavements but not off your clothing and every layer becomes sodden. Jake quietly reassigned his visits to another day and decided to catch up on paperwork and telephone calls. Paperwork in Social Services is always a problem; there is never enough time to write up what work has been done and it is an absolute duty to do it. Jake would generally assign a Tuesday to commit himself to pen-pushing, unless, as often happened, he was interrupted with a more urgent task. Strangely enough, all tasks suddenly take on a certain urgency when the alternative is the completion of running records or assessment forms. But if you don't do it, it will always happen that a crisis will occur or there will be some publicity on one of your cases and you'll find yourself facing disciplinary action for apparently not having done the work. If you write too much, they pick you up on a specific word, or ask exactly why a phrase is written in a particular way. It is a fine balance. As in the rest of social work. And never enough time. A quick phone call first.

'Children Services Admin, Dawn speaking.' Awfully American and new. Have a nice day, Thanksgiving Turkey, Mom's Apple Pie and God Bless Children Services Admin, Jake thought before replying,

'Jake Atkinson, City West. I'm looking for a foster placement for a fifteen-year old boy.'

'Putting you through to Fostering Duty,' and Greensleeves on flat Stylophone drifted down the telephone line. Jake listened to the sound of the rain, which seemed to fall in time to the unpleasant drone on the telephone line and he thought of Daley, desperately hoping that they may come up with a foster place for him. Unlikely for a boy of fifteen. If their parents don't want them, who else will?

His train of thought was broken by a loud woman's voice on the line. She had a very broad Midlands accent. 'Dee Smith 'ere. We've no placements. Certainly not for a fifteen-year old. I'll need a fostering referral filled out and it'll be considered at next Wednesday's meeting. Cheers, then.'

And almost as an afterthought, 'Pity he's not black, or we might have been able to do something.' The phone went down.

Jake rang back and listened again to Greensleeves. When he had been put through to Dee again, he began, 'I'm looking for a foster place for a black child...'

Twenty minutes later, he had the prospect of a foster home for Daley and proceeded to ring Beech Lodge.

It was ten o'clock on Friday morning. It was raining heavily and Jake was walking into the Magistrates Courts with Curtis Wilson. As he walked through the door of the court there was the strong sweetly-scented smell of burning cannabis coming from the direction of a group of young men smoking outside.

'Ganja,' Curtis muttered. Jake looked at him, but Curtis's expression showed only worry.

'What d'you think they'll do to me? I didn't do it.'

Curtis had been arrested at Megasave and had spent a night in the cells because his mother had been unable to come to the police station and the Social Services Emergency Duty Team had no-one to send until the early hours of the morning. Usually it would be someone from the Youth Offending Service who attends. It is unlawful for police to interview a child without an appropriate adult present.

Curtis was being charged with affray, theft from Megasave and assaulting one of Megasave's staff with a knife. He said he and two friends had been in Megasave, just joking amongst themselves when two security guards had walked them out to the car park, taken him round the back of the shop and with the help of three male shop assistants had set upon him in a racist attack. His two friends had struggled free and managed to get away. He was angry because none of the Megasave staff had been charged with anything and afraid because he had never been to court before.

'All rise,' the Court Clerk shouted without looking up from his papers. Curtis was visibly shaking with Jake standing next to him. Three elderly magistrates shuffled out of a side door and into their seats and the rest of the court sat down. Jake remained standing and motioned quietly for Curtis to do the same. To Jake's surprise Mr Wheeler was the magistrate in the middle.

At about the same time he recognised Jake and whispered to the clerk, loudly, 'Which is the defendant?'

The clerk pointed to Curtis and added, 'With his social worker, your worship.' In one of a line of seats in front of Curtis and Jake were the prosecuting solicitor and Curtis's defence solicitor, Martin Sullivan.

'Curtis Lenford Wilson,' the Court Clerk began. Curtis nodded, still shaking. 'You are charged in connection with an incident on the 18th of May of Theft, Affray and Assault Occasioning Actual Bodily Harm. How do you plead?'

Martin Sullivan turned and whispered, 'Not Guilty,' to Curtis.

Curtis repeated, 'Not Guilty,' in a cracked voice.

## Four

There were seven dirty coffee cups on Jake's desk as he walked into the office. He thought about them for a minute, then sat down to try and prioritise his tasks for the day. Core Assessment. A huge booklet of a form needed with every child protection investigation. There are three main areas for consideration and within those, twenty in total for a proper assessment of the unmet needs of a child. What worried Jake even more than the time limit in which you have to complete the form was the fact that it has to be done on the computer. First, learn to turn the computer on. Then teach yourself to type. Then work out how long you have to complete the assessment. According to the Department of Health, thirty-five days. According to the Area Safeguarding Board responsible for child protection, fourteen days to Child Protection Conference, which needs to see the assessment. As Jake turned to his computer, Frances' voice called from behind, 'Jake you're to interview Mr Davis with Sally. She needs a man.'

Not this man, Jake thought and turned to see Sally waiting for him in the office doorway.

As Jake walked down the stairs with Sally, he stopped on the landing and asked, 'What information do I need to know about this man?' She looked grim.

'He's allegedly cut off two of his best mate's fingers with a kitchen knife last week, because he wouldn't give him a cigarette. His wife, Moira and her two kids were put into a refuge yesterday with my help, because they came in asking to get away from him, saying he's violent. The Police have interviewed him, but his mate won't press charges. Rumour has it that he thinks pressing charges is like pressing buttons and he's no longer equipped to do that, what with missing a couple of digits. Mr Davis'll be here to ask where his wife and children are. We don't tell him.'

'And my presence?' As if Jake didn't know.

'You're coming with me for protection, so to speak. Frances has this sexist approach that a man can somehow placate Mr Davis better than I can.'

Jake hated this approach. It's always more difficult for a man than a woman in social work. If a violent man is going to threaten a social worker, they generally will stop short of hitting a woman, unless they are mentally ill. A man's a better target. Men have to be much better talkers than women when it comes to calming people down. Jake's approach was generally to ensure he was sitting down, with access to an exit and to lower his voice, speaking more slowly and quietly the angrier they became. And to ensure they knew he was telling the truth. It generally worked.

As they approached the interview room through reception, a red-faced figure in a donkey jacket stood up and sneered in a Glaswegian accent, 'Brought protection with you, eh? You'll need it.'

Sally and Jake walked into the interview room, each taking a seat either side of the door.

'How can we help you, Mr Davis?' Sally began.

'I want to know where's my wife and wains? You've removed them, haven't you?' Sally looked him in the eye.

'Can I ask you a question before I answer, Mr Davis?'

'Go on.'

'Which would you prefer? An absolutely honest answer to your question or a nice pleasant answer which will tell you nothing?'

Robert Davis, Known as Rab or Rabbie to his friends (whose numbers were reputedly dwindling), looked up surprised. He thought for a minute before answering.

'I'd rather have the truth; give me it straight, that's what I'd prefer.'

'Well then,' said Sally, discreetly taking a deep breath, 'this is the absolute truth. We have assisted your wife and your two children. We have put them in touch with the Women's Refuge Services and they have been taken away to a secret location. I'm sorry but I am not in a position to give you any information about where that might be but it is likely that they will eventually be in touch with you if they choose to. You have the right to go to a Solicitor and apply to a Court to get access to your children.'

Sally sat back and Jake watched Rab Davis. Rab Davis sat and thought quietly for some two minutes. Those two minutes seemed like an eternity.

Eventually he looked up and said, 'I appreciate you being straight; people aren't often straight with me. Mebbe they're afraid of me.'

As Jake watched him thinking, he noticed his hands. L O V E on the right hand and H A T on the left hand with the little finger blank. No E. Jake wondered what had happened there. Could he not spell? Did he run out of money? Did he run out of ink? Did it hurt too much? Had he had a finger graft? Maybe he'd fallen in love with a girl called Harriet or he loved hats. Perhaps his friend's finger had the missing E. Whichever way it was most unusual. Perhaps he preferred L O V E  H A T to L O V E on one and H A T E on the other. Whatever the reason, it was not the sort of question Jake felt he ought to ask at this particular time and in these particular circumstances.

After Rab Davis had given his response to Sally he just sat. As he sat his eyes welled up with tears. 'I can't live without my kids you know and I do love them.'

Sally said, 'We understand. These situations are always difficult and it's always better if we can tackle them honestly. What I will do is I will get a message to your wife and children that you've come in to ask about them.'

He said, 'Would you give them another message?'

'And what would that be?'

Rab Davies said in a hoarse whisper, 'Tell them I love them.'

'I'll do that.'

Jake looked across at Sally. He saw her in a new light; she'd handled that interview with skill, with care and with honesty. It had been one in which she'd had the potential to feel threatened. He also realised that she had of course been correct in implying that his presence shouldn't be necessary. He would remember it for next time.

As they went upstairs Jake said to Sally, 'I'm impressed, Sally. I thought you did that really well.'

Sally turned and smiled, a little surprised. 'Thanks, Jake, I appreciate that,' as they returned to their desks.

Across town, Tom Davey stood between the pillars in front of the door of a very large house. He didn't like making Child Protection Enquiries, particularly those involving posh families. Pressing the doorbell, he was surprised to hear it play a very flat 'Happy Birthday' inside the house. Tacky, but you can't tell a gift by the wrapping.

As the door opened, he tried to look his most professional. 'Mrs Devonshire?' He spoke in almost a whisper. 'I'm Tom Davey, from the Council's Children's Services. May I have a word?'

'What about?' Cressida Devonshire was the same age as Tom at 47 and the first thing he noticed was a Liberty's silk square round her neck with the knot to one side. It didn't really match the pink Elle T-shirt and black pink-trimmed joggers with a Playboy label. She was barefoot.

'You can speak here. I don't think I've got any business with Social Services and if you're trying to sell anything in aid of the disabled I'm not interested.' Very Penelope Keith accent.

'Actually Mrs Devonshire, it's slightly more serious than that. If you're sure you want to speak on the doorstep in the potential hearing of your neighbours, then I'm pleased to do so. It's about your daughter Lucinda, who, we understand, is fifteen.'

Tom thought he saw, out of the corner of his eye the curtain twitch on the front window of the house to his right. In spite of the impressive portico and fake Georgian bays, these modern houses were remarkably close together.

'It's Ms Devonshire. I suppose you'd better come in.'

The door opened and Tom stepped into a laminate-floored hallway, on which his trainers squeaked. Cressida Devonshire walked straight through into the kitchen.

'Coffee or tea? And have you any identity?'

'Coffee, white with two sugars, please.' From a deep side pocket in his khaki cargoes, he produced a well-worn identity card.

He sipped the milky Nescafé slowly and took a deep breath. 'We have a report that you've just returned from a week's holiday in Italy.'

'Tuscany and Calabria, actually. Florence, or as we call it, Firenze is more attractive in the Autumn, in the lead up to Christmas, but it's lovely at every time of the year.' Perhaps more Hyacinth Bucket than Penelope Keith on second thoughts.

'Our concern is that we understand Lucinda was left here on her own during that time and she's not sixteen until the summer.'

'So I get visited by the Social Police to pass judgement on my lifestyle?' Her voice was getting louder and she pointed as she spoke. 'I'll have you know this is not a welfare family and my daughter is a highly responsible and mature young lady. She doesn't attend comprehensive school.' She spat the word 'comprehensive' out disdainfully. 'And I am not without influence. Get out. You will be hearing from my solicitors. And they're not a tin pot firm either. Out.' Her voice had risen to a shriek.

Tom Davey wasted no time squeaking across the hall floor and was breathless by the time he reached his car.

For the second time in two days, Tom Davey stood between the pillars in front of the door of a very large house. Next to him was a smart looking Asian woman in a dark suit over which was a black quilted coat.

Frances had been furious on Tom's return the day before. 'Child protection is child protection. I've changed my mind and I'll have a full core assessment. Take the Police with you if you have to, but not doing it is not an option.'

Tom had inwardly groaned. Core Assessments take up to seven weeks and involve several visits. He needed a toilet. Urgently. He had excused himself with indecent haste.

The door opened and Cressida Devonshire took stock. That scraggy social worker had the temerity to return. This time he had a female assistant. Asian and dressed up like a dog's dinner.

She raised herself to her full height. 'I thought I had made it entirely clear,' she began.

The Dog's Dinner opened a wallet, showing a Police badge. 'Detective Constable Kamaljit Kaur,' she said quietly, 'It's in your best interests to talk to us, Mrs Devonshire.' No coffee this time. Opening the door into the lounge, Cressida Devonshire motioned them to a floral sofa and took a seat on a recliner opposite.

The policewoman had an air of quiet authority. 'These are formal enquiries under Section 47 of the Children Act 1989. We have an allegation of neglect in that you have been away on holiday for a week leaving your fifteen year old daughter, Lucinda Fiona Devonshire alone without a responsible adult to look after her. At this stage charges are not necessarily to be brought, but if you wish to avoid formal action, I must advise you that you should cooperate fully with Mr Davey here.'

It was not a long discussion. Cressida Devonshire agreed to make several appointments for Tom to visit and fill out an assessment. She was left in no doubt that it is not appropriate to go abroad leaving your daughter alone, even if she is a mature fifteen and an A grade student.

Kam Kaur was not impressed with Tom Davey. His spineless approach had done him no credit. However, as far as she was concerned, it shouldn't merit any further action and for her part it was a job well done.

As Jake walked into Beech Lodge he could hear the sound of a struggle. Just outside one of the main bedrooms in a corridor, there was what looked like a rugby scrum, with four members of staff holding someone down. As he approached, he saw Monnie bend over and take the hand of the person underneath.

'Well, bless me, I've never seen a palm like it – I've got to tell your fortune now, before another minute passes. Let him go, get off, get off.'

The muffled shouts from the restrained body stopped and, one by one, the staff members gingerly got up. As Monnie helped the ruffled figure to his feet, Jake was amazed to see it was Daley. Monnie took Daley's hand and he obligingly let her lead him, as meek as a new-born lamb. Monnie winked at Jake and pointing a finger at her ear motioned him to listen from outside as they entered Daley's bedroom.

'You've not had an easy life. Let me see, this hand tells me your Mum doesn't always appreciate you. You've recently met someone who isn't kind to you either – would that be a friend of your Mum's?'

Jake sneaked a look through the half open door to see Monnie sitting on the bed with Daley and both of them studying his right hand.

'Now I've said a bit, it's your turn to tell me why you hate it here enough to start a ruckus like that.' Jake heard Daley sniff and sob,

'They told me I've got to go to a foster home and I don't want to leave here.'

'Why would that be?' Monnie asked, genuinely perplexed.

Daley looked down at his shoes. At the same time a quiet voice behind Jake whispered, 'Because he's shagging Alison Bryant, that's why.'

Jake turned to see two young people behind him, watching intently. As he turned, they both nodded. Two girls, about twelve, both with straggly blond hair with pink tips were standing behind him. There were no staff to be seen. One of the girls, Kylie, in regulation Adidas Poppers and a FCUK T-shirt had a stud through her nose, reddened and weeping at the side of her left nostril. Her shoes were strappy once-white follow-me-home-and-fuck-me sandals a size or two too big for her. Her friend, Elle, had a denim skirt so short it just revealed a pair of dirty pink knickers. Her Reebok trainers looked new and a boob tube just covered the beginnings of breasts. Both girls looked unkempt and unwashed.

'I said,' this time louder from FCUK, 'it's because he's shagging Alison Bryant.' Jake glanced into Daley's bedroom, to see him angrily turn towards the door and go a bright red colour. Something about Daley's instant discomfort made Jake feel extremely uneasy. He looked for Monnie's reaction, but she appeared not to have heard it. Jake quietly approached Daley, as Monnie got up,

'Now then girls, what mischief have you got for me?' Monnie approached the girls, smiled and followed them down the corridor. Jake sat on the bed next to Daley.

'Is it true?' he asked. Daley continued to look at his feet, brought his knees to his chest and put his thumb in his mouth. His face remained a deep red colour. Jake sat with him for fifteen minutes. The only response he had was when he asked Daley if he'd rather be left alone and Daley silently nodded. Jake left.

Monica O'Leary's ability to read a situation had nothing at all to do with foreseeing the future or reading palms. She had been born Monica Kilkelly in County Clare, the daughter of a farmer. A clever and beautiful young woman, she had originally been intending to study veterinary surgery. For some reason she had opted instead to work with people and studied psychology and English literature, graduating with a first in both from Trinity College in Dublin in the 1970s. She had been a successful practising clinical psychologist in Galway until she was in her thirties and met Pat O'Leary, a London based engineer of Irish origin. They eventually married and moved first to Dollis Hill in North West London. Three children later, they moved north to Nottinghamshire and Monica did a conversion course to qualify as a British social worker at Nottingham University. She never told her colleagues about her previous qualifications and used her language skills and timing to deflect the discrimination she encountered against the Irish. Her diversion tactics worked and she was renowned as a woman with bad language and a good sense of humour. Often as a result of her charm, people forgot she was Irish, making life a great deal easier than it might have been. In Daley's case however, her uncannily accurate analysis was not so much based on her background as a psychologist as on the fact that Jake had told her all about Daley the previous day in the office.

It was a glorious summer day with a cloudless sky as Sarah wheeled Harley into the hospital clinic waiting room at a quarter-to-three. She knew she would have at least a fifteen-minute wait to see Dr Gohil and planned to make productive use of the time. To her secret disappointment, there were no other patients waiting. She sat on one of the soft blue seats facing the baby. Harley strained to get out of his chair as Sarah reached into her shopping bag on the back and took out a four-fingered Kit-Kat. His eyes eager with anticipation and his chin wet, he chuckled and gurgled as he reached forward. Sarah was midway through her second finger when she recognised his request and wrapping the end of the half finger in some silver foil, she gave it to him. He slurped noisily, grunting with satisfaction. He was still doing so as she broke off the fourth finger of the chocolate and stopped stock-still. What if they didn't have a clinic today? Supposing they had set up an appointment just for her? What were they wanting to see her about anyway? She was sure she hadn't got the day wrong. She pulled the crumpled appointment letter from her bag and double-checked it. As her Kit Kat melted itself round her fingers, she thought of an excellent idea.

As Sarah took Harley into the baby changing room, Jake was walking into the hospital main entrance. He had a small teddy bear crammed into his trouser pocket. He'd been given it with petrol points from filling his car on his way over and thought Harley would like it. He'd spent some considerable time fiddling with it to make sure the eyes wouldn't come off and choke a baby. His purpose in visiting was to support Sarah and see to it that the Consultant understood the level of stress she was under as a result of uncertainty with Harley's condition. Every time she was at appointments, he reflected, her anxiety affected the child, so that he appeared a very unsettled youngster when medical staff saw him. They'd also seen his fits, which Jake hadn't. He wondered if the mother's anxiety might in some way be linked to the baby's fits, which seemed to happen more frequently outside the home. There might be a link, which he briefly thought he must have been missing. No doubt, he thought, it would become clear eventually.

Sarah had by now almost completed her Special Hug. As she had planned, after he quietened, she just held onto the Hug a couple of seconds extra and then a couple more. As she screamed and carried the little slumped figure out to the waiting area he was just a little bluer than usual. He still had Kit Kat round his mouth.

Jake was running. Up the hill by the side of the Arboretum. Change of pace needed to stretch a bit. Quietly copying American soldiers, he began chanting to himself, to run in time, 'One two three four, Ricky's face is at the door. Five six seven eight, hope my visit's not too late....'

He couldn't get it out of his head and as he approached St Andrew's Road, almost home, a woman in jeans and a tee-shirt rounded the corner and, unable to stop quickly enough, he ran into her, knocking her over. He stopped,

'I really am most terribly sorry. Are you okay? Here, let me help you up.' He offered his hand as an embarrassed and familiar face looked up. 'It's Alison Bryant, isn't it?'

'I'm fine thanks Jake, if a little winded.' She took his hand and stood up.

As she brushed herself down Jake felt very guilty. He apologized again and said, 'Will you be alright and is there anything I can do?'

Alison looked up and offered a half smile and said coyly, 'That'll cost you a drink sometime, Jake,' rising to her feet. 'or should I call you Rambo, mowing people down like that?' Jake smiled and relaxed a little.

'I'd be more than happy to oblige. I'd offer now, except I'm hardly dressed for it,' and he looked down at his running shorts. 'However, I only live round the corner and if you need to...' He suddenly felt embarrassed and couldn't find the words.

'I was on my way home, so I wouldn't mind a cup of coffee,' Alison said shyly and added, 'no talking shop, though.'

'I'll just get cleaned up. Coffee, tea, can of Stella? Or I've even got some red wine.' They were in Jake's kitchen. Alison was sitting in a chair at the breakfast bar and Jake was filling a kettle from the tap. 'If you want you can turn on the telly in the lounge while I shower and change. The Grumpies are on, if you like that sort of thing.'

'The Grumpies?' asked Alison.

'EastEnders. A programme about several dysfunctional Cockney families who all winge and argue constantly. I'd never live in London, they're all so miserable. Come to that, Coronation Street's the same, so is Emmerdale, just with different accents.' Alison laughed out loud at Jake's analysis of television soap opera.

'Actually, I like EastEnders and it's about real life. Having given it some thought, I'll have a cup of coffee and recover from having been assaulted by some half-dressed macho male while you're getting changed.'

Jake let the shower begin to chill him out. He was thinking about Alison. Blonde, five foot five, a nice shape and really quite attractive. Sense of humour and bright too. He hoped she'd spend some time. Maybe she'd like something to eat. He slipped into a pair of Wranglers and a cord shirt and went down to see her, just as EastEnders was finishing. 'Recovered? I'll buy you that drink if you like.' Alison smiled in assent.

As they got to the door of the Manor Arms public house, Jake opened the door for Alison to walk in first. She chose the inner door labeled 'Snug' and walked in.

Jake followed. 'What can I get you?'

'I think I'll have a Bacardi and Diet Coke,' said Alison, 'I don't have to drive anywhere.' Alison chose one of the many tables in the Beer Garden, or Smoker's Yard as it had become known, while Jake went to the bar where he bought himself a pint of draught Guinness and for her a double Bacardi and Coke.

Fishing in his pocket he brought out a large handful of loose change and said to Christine the Liverpudlian barmaid, 'Sorry about the shrapnel.'

'That's alright dear, we like change,' she said, smiling and leaning slightly forward as she did so. Jake tried not to notice that Christine had a black, greasy line of dandruff at the centre parting in her hair and that the bra that was visible to him needed a wash.

He took the drinks and walked back to the table. The walls of the Snug in the Manor Arms were a dark cream colour from years of nicotine stains. There were beams across the ceiling all surprisingly uniform and some with a small gap where they were supposed to meet the main beam in the centre of the ceiling.

Jake joined Alison at the outside table and sat down. 'Mind if I smoke?' he asked, taking a box of Villigers out of the pocket of his leather jacket and putting them on the table.

'What's a runner like you doing smoking?' asked Alison.

'Enjoying each and every one,' responded Jake with a smile and retorted, 'what's a nice slim girl like you putting Diet Coke in her Bacardi for?' Alison said, 'Me, slim? I wish! I'm far too fat.'

'I wouldn't bother with the Diet Coke,' said Jake, 'you can't improve on perfection.'

Alison blushed slightly and chuckled, looking down to brush an imaginary speck of fluff from her jeans. She reached into her bag and took out a packet of Benson and Hedges and a small Zippo lighter.

Jake looked at it curiously. 'Is that a Zippo?'

'Certainly is, ladies' special.'

'I've never seen a Zippo that small,' replied Jake. Alison responded, 'You leave my Zippo out of this until later,' and giggled adding, 'anyway, size isn't everything – at least that's what men normally tell me.' They were both silent for a short while.

'So what's your passion in life? What interests you?' asked Jake.

Alison looked at him. 'I don't know really; I spend so much of my time at work and we've decided we're not going to discuss work. I suppose if I were to write an advert about myself it would be Likes Theatre, Wining And Dining, Clubbing, Reading, Quite Sporty and Likes Something Unusual, a Bit of Adventure. And you?'

Jake thought before answering. 'I suppose it'd be Music, Cooking, Travel and as you know I'm keen on running, especially when I can bump into nice young women.' Alison laughed.

'That was quite an introduction wasn't it? What does one say…fancy bumping into you like that?' Jake smiled and nodded towards Alison's glass. Alison lit her cigarette,

'And what do you really dislike?'

Jake half smiled. 'Intercourse smoking.'

'Why? There's nothing like a whiff of nicotine after you've... not that I ever have, but I've been told about it,' she quickly added and looked down, coyly.

'I reckon,' retorted Jake, 'that if someone lights up after my prawn cocktail, it puts me right off my Boeuf Bourguignon.'

After they finished laughing, Jake looked at his watch, 'Do you fancy another?'

Alison said, 'I'll buy, it's my round.'

'No,' said Jake, 'I insist, I was the one that knocked you over.'

'Alright,' replied Alison, 'I'll have a Bacardi and Diet Coke.' She smiled, remembering the remark earlier about perfection and wondering whether Jake actually fancied her or whether he was naturally flirty.

'How did you get into Social work?' Jake asked as he returned to their table.

'I wanted to be a Doctor but didn't get the A levels,' said Alison, 'so I thought it was perhaps the next best thing. I wish I hadn't now. I'd rather have been anything other than a Social Worker. It's a thankless job.'

Jake nodded in agreement, 'Yes, I'd go with that. Somehow you can never do it right.'

Alison asked, 'I know it's on the subject of work, but can I enquire, do you get along with Frances Phillips?'

Jake looked puzzled. 'I'm not sure how to answer that one; I don't think I know her well enough yet.' He was a bit guarded in his response. Frances had given him the impression that she and Alison were best mates.

Alison continued, 'I can't stand her, the two-faced cow!'

Jake relaxed, 'Thank goodness for that. I didn't feel as if I could trust her very much but one is reluctant to say at such times.'

Alison smiled. 'Oh, your secret's safe with me. I'm a Social Worker. You can always trust me,' and they both laughed.

As Jake got to the bar and put the glasses down, Christine approached and gave him a wide smile showing clear black lines between her teeth giving her mouth the appearance of a misshapen Bechstein.

'That's alright dear; I'll give you clean ones.' She winked at him and licked her lips. Her eye lashes were almost stuck together with heavy mascara and her lipstick was a gaudy, almost orange colour some of which had transferred itself to her front teeth. 'What'll it be this time?' she said, once again leaning forward in that familiar way to show Jake her grubby once white, now grey bra.

'Another pint of Guinness and double Bacardi with Diet Coke please,' said Jake. As Christine turned away to get Jake his drinks, a man sitting on a bar stool with his back to Jake turned around.

'Ey up Jake.'

'Hello Ernie.' Ernie was eighty two years of age, a large man with a pendulous stomach hanging over his belt.

'That's a reet cracker yer've pulled there, is she free?'

Jake smiled. 'No, I'm buying her double Bacardis.'

'Ee, I used to pull crackers like that when I wore an owd boy,' Ernie reflected. 'So did you didn't yer Alf?' Another old man sitting next to Ernie turned round. 'D'ya know Alf, me mate? He's a good youth. We was at school together and in the war and down't pits. 'E got Vibrator White Finger.' A smile and a cough from both of them. 'And now we're on us pensions.'

Alf nodded and gave a broad, gummy smile. 'That Ernie,' he said, ''e's 'ed more 'ot dinners than yo've 'ed women,' he said, nodding towards Ernie's stomach. Both men chuckled bronchitically.

Ernie leaned across and gave a loud whisper to Jake, 'Ayer blobbed 'er? There's nowt like a nice piece of raw liver round yer lips. Wi' gravy,' he added and the two old men wheezed with laughter till they coughed. As they did so they raised their pints to their lips to wash the emphysema back down.

'It's us bronicals,' by way of explanation.

Jake raised his eyebrows and said to them, in a mock serious tone, 'Time gentlemen please.'

'Only a joke duck,' said Ernie.

'Ar surry,' said Alf, 'we di'n't mean nowt by it.'

Christine put the two filled glasses on the bar. Jake's clean glass had a large lipstick mark at the top of it. Jake picked it up.

'Does the lipstick come for free?'

'Sorry duck,' said Christine and promptly poured the drink into the glass Jake had brought back earlier and put on the bar.

Jake made his way back to the table with the drinks. What with old men being youths and youngsters being owd boys round here it's hard to know where you stand, he mused.

Back at the table he gently slid Alison's drink across to her. 'There you go,' he said.

'You're a gent,' she replied. 'Bottoms up. Yours first.' And peering theatrically at the side of his jeans, she chortled.

The juke box crackled into life and an old Elvis song came up. Jake caught some words *'Cos if there's one thing that she don't need it's another little hungry mouth to feed...'* and his thoughts went back again to Ricky and

Ryan. He suddenly became aware that Alison had asked him a question and looked up.

'Eh? Sorry?'

'I said where did you qualify?'

'Sheffield,' said Jake

'Oh, with bonking Bill the lecherer?'

'Yes,' said Jake, 'I've heard stories about broom cupboards and female students with him.'

'The trouble is,' said Alison, 'the floor brush spikes get up your nose.' And she laughed. *'And his mama cries...'* from the juke box. And Jake thought I bet Daley's Mama did too. His thoughts were interrupted again.

'You seem a bit distracted,' said Alison.

'Well,' said Jake slowly, 'I've got a lot on at the moment. I'm not finding my colleagues ever so supportive, except Monnie,' he added.

'Fuck off O'Leary?' said Alison, 'she's a card isn't she? I don't know how she gets away with it.' Jake nodded and took a drink. From the juke box, *'And he learned how to steal and he learned how to fight...'* and Jake thought, *and play cricket maybe.* Determined to change his thought process Jake turned to Alison and said, 'What about your family? Any brothers, sisters?'

'I don't know,' said Alison, 'I grew up in foster care. I didn't like it but it's not something I really like to talk about.' Jake suddenly wondered whether there was more to Alison's past than he had previously imagined. He'd seen her as a middle-class teenager growing up in suburbia with maybe one or two siblings. Perhaps there was more to her than met the eye.

'Well, what would you like to tell me about yourself?' he asked.

'I can tell you I've got a nickname,' Alison replied.

'What's that?' said Jake.

'Rosie,' said Alison.

'Why's that?' said Jake.

'Because of my delicacy, grace and natural beauty,' said Alison. The Bacardis were making her less reserved. 'And there might be another reason,' she added, fluttering her eyelashes.

'Such as?'

'TMI,' she shot back. Jake looked puzzled.

'Too Much Information. How long have you been running?' she asked, changing the subject.

'Oh, for about five years now,' said Jake.

'Ever done the Marathon?'

'Just once. It hurts.'

Alison was interested, 'Oh, I always fancied doing that; you run over the finishing line and everybody's cheering and thinking you're great.'

'Believe me, by the time you get to the finishing line you don't feel great. Last time, the only time I ran a marathon, it was the Nottingham. They call it the Robin Hood and it was sponsored by a pork pie factory. I got to the end feeling sick and drained and they gave me a voucher for a pig flesh pie. Luverley.' In a Jamie Oliver accent.

'Oh!' said Alison, 'you would have thought they'd have given you something better than that. Fish and chips, maybe.'

'Well,' said Jake, 'you also get a nice piece of lace in a frame.'

Alison said, 'Is that all? For running twenty-three miles?'

'Twenty-six actually,' said Jake, 'and three hundred and eighty-five yards. And by the time you get to eighteen you feel as though you're going to die and at around the twenty-three mile marker you wish your end would just come quickly. By the time you get to twenty-six… well, I tell you when I got to twenty-six miles they had to roof-rack me home.'

Alison laughed at the prospect, 'So you won't be doing it again then?'

'Oh, I'm not sure about that,' said Jake. 'Thinking about it, I quite fancy doing the London or maybe the New York.'

'You get some sponsorship to do the New York and I'll come and watch you.'

'That's a deal,' said Jake. 'Ready for another drink?'

Alison said, 'I'll need to visit the little girl's room first.'

As she shimmied across the front of the bar, Jake thought, 'She's a nice shape,' and then thought, *raw liver*, and shuddered.

Jake had returned from the bar with his fourth pint of Guinness and Alison's fourth Bacardi with Diet Coke by the time she came out from the toilet. Jake noticed her make-up had been refreshed and somehow her teeth looked whiter than before. As she walked across the bar towards him he thought, s*he really is quite an attractive woman.*

'Nice name, Alison. You know Chaucer called a lot of his women Alison?'

'I hate it.' Alison replied. 'I'd much sooner have a more modern name.'

'Chardonnay, maybe? Did you ever watch that old TV programme, Footballer's Wives? It's being repeated on Freeview.' To his surprise, Alison burst out laughing.

'What?' he asked.

'I liked it. The programme anyway. It just occurred to me that if you were going to call your baby after a bottle of wine, it could have been Bull's Blood or Blue Nun, or…' She was unable to continue for laughing.

Some minutes later, she spluttered in between snorts of laughter, 'A friend gave me a bottle of wine called The Dog's Bollocks. Can you imagine? Dad, I want you to meet my new girlfriend…' She couldn't finish as they both were laughing so much.

By the time Alison had had her fourth Bacardi and Jake his fourth pint they were both beginning to feel hungry.

Alison said, 'Do you fancy something to eat? I'm ravishing.'

Jake replied, 'I wouldn't disagree with that.'

'With what?' asked Alison.

'That I could fancy something to eat.' Jake had a mischievous smile on his face. Alison gave a half smile and looked at him under her lashes, dark with mascara.

'Why don't you come back to mine?' said Jake 'and I'll cook you something.'

'Done,' replied Alison, adding with a cheeky grin, 'are there no end to your talents?' With that they put their coats on and left.

Jake felt that slight lightness in the head and heaviness in the stomach that four pints of Draught Guinness brings on. The air had a slight chill about it. As they walked past the Arboretum, Alison slipped her hand into Jake's.

'Fancy some chips? I could eat an 'oss 'tween two mattresses,' she said in a Mansfield accent. Jake laughed.

'Where were you thinking of eating it?' Alison was four Bacardi and Cokes less shy than earlier,

'I'd invite you back to mine, up Redcliffe, but it's in too much of a state for visitors.'

Jake began, hesitantly, 'As I said earlier, if you want to risk my cooking, I can rustle up a Carbonara at mine…'

By the time they arrived at Jake's home Alison had her arm through Jake's. As they got to the front door Jake reached into his pocket for his key, turned towards the door and in doing so lightly brushed across Alison's breast. Slightly embarrassed he turned to apologise only to find she was closer than he expected. Somehow their lips met and they were kissing, long and slowly on the doorstep.

Jake opened the door to the lounge and they both fell onto the sofa in the lounge still entwined.

As they stopped for air, Alison asked, 'How d'you feel about tattoos?'

'I don't if they're on sailors.'

'And if they're on a special part of a girl who fancies you?'

'Like where?'

'You might find out if you're lucky.' She moved her hand up his thigh and, feeling how hard he was under his jeans, whispered, 'If I'm lucky…'

Some ten minutes later, Jake's shirt was unbuttoned and Alison's was partly undone as they grappled on the sofa.

Jake paused. 'Food.'

'I could pass on it,' mumbled Alison, almost into Jake's mouth. Jake sat up, untying his legs from Alison's.

'Ten-minute specials. Trust me. I'm an Alpha Male.' In the kitchen he put some spaghetti on to boil and eight minutes later brought in two bowls of Carbonara and two glasses of red wine.

After they finished eating, Alison took the bowls and glasses and put them in the sink. As she walked back to the sofa, she let out a long sigh of satisfaction, adding, 'Gorgeous.'

'You old flatterer,' smiled Jake, 'still, I do try to look after myself.'

'No, the snap, you wally.' And putting her arms round him she kissed him full on the lips. As they pulled apart, she whispered, 'You can show me your bedroom if you like.'

Alison had woken Jake at six. 'I've got to go to mine and get changed. Ring me.' And was gone.

Jake couldn't stop thinking about Alison while driving to work. Not so much about Alison, but her pubic rose. Why would anyone have a tattoo there? Who would she plan to show it to? What was the tattooist like who did it? Did she go in and ask the cost of a flower on her fanny, a bloom on her growler? Had he deflowered her after planting her rose? There seemed something altogether out of the ordinary in such a normal, nice woman walking around with a rose adorning her mons pubis. His pattern of thought was interrupted by a motorcyclist speeding past him.

'Organ donor,' he muttered, as he pulled into Social Services car park, to see a new dent on the front wing of

Monica's Ford Focus, which had been reverse-parked across two parking bays.

# Five

Alison Bryant clocked off her shift. She was lost in thought as she walked home. It had been during just such a walk that Jake had run into her. Literally. She smiled at the memory. She really liked Jake. He was different. Most men she had encountered weren't interested in anything other than getting inside her pants. Not that she usually minded. Alison had needs. Didn't all women? It's not something you talk about. Her needs might have been more than some. God knows she'd started early enough, with being taken away from her parents at the age of three. She was always told they were not good parents.

She remembered, though. Dad would repeatedly flick the top of one of those ballpoint pens where you pushed the button to make the point come out. That was the signal. Her older sister, Sadie would take her upstairs by the hand and they would both get undressed and wait in their beds for Dad to come into the bedroom. Sadie would be lying in her own bed and Alison in hers, with her My Little Pony bedding. Dad came in and lay in Sadie's bed with Sadie under the sheets. Alison had watched as he lifted Sadie on top of him. Then when Sadie started crying as she always did, Dad would come into her bed. He always did the same thing, sticking his finger inside her bits, then shaking himself until he wet her leg. He would sometimes give her some sweets before he went back downstairs.

She didn't know what had happened to Sadie. The last contact she'd had with her sister had been three years prior when Sadie had traced her and contacted her to ask for money. Sadie at that time was living in Leeds in a squat. She had come across to visit and had looked terrible. Alison could see she had a habit but hadn't asked the sister she'd admired as an infant. Her habit was probably heroin or could be crack cocaine, but Alison didn't want to know. Sadie was only two years older than Alison, but looked ten or more. She had looked as if she was on the game as well. Alison had given her fifty pounds and sent her on her way.

Reflecting on it now, she realised what a filthy and perverse man her father must have been. She never saw him after she went into foster care with the Davidsons. Thinking back they hadn't been bad foster parents until she was twelve and her body began to change. Jack Davidson was a security man and used to drive from bank to bank. It was when she was twelve that he started to take her with him in the school holidays and it was in the board room upstairs in one of his banks that he offered to get her a new bike if she would keep a secret. The secret was that he would touch her and kiss between her legs and she would rub between his. She got her bike. And a stereo, a television of her own and anything else she asked for. And she kept the secret. She wasn't sure whether she had consented to what had happened or not. But it kept happening until she was sixteen and left the Davidsons. It had changed over the years from masturbating him to full sex. She got used to it and it would give her a peculiar pleasure she could never describe on the odd occasion she reached a climax. She reflected that the pleasure was never in any way to do with Jack Davidson, but all to do with a physical reaction, which she eventually discovered she could achieve by herself.

Her thoughts were interrupted as she passed the top of Jake's road. She wondered what he was doing at the moment. She could imagine him becoming her first serious boyfriend, after years of casual relationships. Jake had everything. He was good-looking, had a great personality, good sense of humour and could even cook. Pretty good in bed as well. She'd see how it worked out.

Duty officer Monica O'Leary picked up the phone. It was twenty-past two and a busy Monday.

'It's Sue on reception. I've got a Child Protection referral.'

'Anyone we know?'

'I'm not sure if you've dealt with the family before, but we regularly get them. Name of Hegarty.'

'Not Roy and Marie Hegarty in Thorpe Park?'

'That's the one. It's the nursery Ryan goes to. They say he's got an inflicted injury on his arm. Ryan's quite proud of it and has been showing everyone, saying his Dad hit him with a belt.'

'Feck. I'm on my way. I'll speak to Frances first then go straight over.'

'Frances, I need an urgent word.' Monnie hovered in the doorway. 'I've just picked up a Section 47 on the Hegarty family. I've just spoken to Stafford Nursery and young Ryan's got a mark on his arm. He's saying his dad's hit him with a belt.'

Frances ushered Monnie in and closed the door. 'It's not like Roy to take a belt to the kids. They've only recently buried Ricky and from what I heard they were looking after the others brilliantly. Knowing Roy and how aggressive he can be, are you going with the Police or do you want another social worker with you?'

'I'd rather go on my own.' Monica looked determined. 'They know me and they won't mess me about. If I take someone else he'll never tell me what's happened, but if you'll get someone to set up an appointment with the hospital so I can take him straight to the paediatrician, it'll let me get over there pronto.'

'I'll see to it.' Frances was pleased with Monica's approach. Monica was a steely woman when it was necessary. 'Take an office cell phone. I'll stay at my desk until you ring in to tell me what's happened. Oh and take some core assessment forms. It'll have to be a Child Protection Conference what with the other twin dying recently.'

Monica scurried out.

Marie was looking anxiously out of the window as Monica pulled up outside the house, her alloy wheel grating against the kerb. As she approached the open front door, she heard a familiar voice shout, 'We're having nothing to do with 'king welfare. Fuck off back to your office.'

Undaunted, Monica walked in through the open front door and called, 'Now then Roy, that's no way to greet an elderly woman and one like yourself from the old country.'

'Oh, it's Mrs O'Leary.' Roy appeared from the kitchen at the back. 'I thought they'd sent one of the nasty bastards when Marie said the Welfare was here.'

'And less of the bad language. Those are my colleagues you're talking about. Now then, Roy and Marie, can I come in properly and sit down?' Monnie moved into the lounge and remained standing. 'I think you probably know why I'm here. I've had a call from the nursery. Let's get down to business.'

Roy and Marie Hegarty sat on the sofa, Marie holding Stevie-Lee, the baby. Monica looked, steely-eyed at Roy. 'Ryan's got an injury. Who's going to tell me what happened? Before you do, I'll tell you now that I'm to take him and the baby to the hospital to be looked at. I'd like you both to come with me.'

Roy and Marie Hegarty both looked first at each other then at the floor, before Roy asked, 'And where's this so-called injury supposed to be? Don't you think we deserve to be left in peace with what we've recently gone through with Ricky?' His eyes were full of tears and Marie began to sob at the mention of Ricky's name.

'God knows you've suffered and I feel for you, but you've got to understand that we're not allowed to ignore a call like this from the nursery. The boy's got a mark on his arm according to what I've been told and he's told the nursery his version of how it happened. Now do you want to tell me yours?'

Roy began to cry. 'If I tell you straight, we'll lose him. You'll take him away and we'll have lost both. Please. Mrs O'Leary I beg you not to do this. Please.'

Monica, still steely-eyed sat down in the chair opposite. 'If you don't tell me, everyone will assume you're guilty and you might lose the baby as well. And that's before the Police decide whether to prosecute or not. I'm not going to lie to you. You know the score.'

'What's Ryan said? What are we supposed to have done?' It was a quiet, but insistent voice from Marie.

'No, Marie, I won't tell you that at this time. If you don't know about the injury on Ryan's arm, we'll go and see the Doctor and he'll give us an idea of how it might have been done.' Monica stood up. 'Which one's coming with the baby, or will it be both? Have you got nappies and his coat?'

'No, wait.' This time it was Roy who spoke. 'I'll tell you. It'll sound really stupid.'

'Good lad, Roy. I'm listening.' Monica sat back down again.

'It was on Saturday afternoon. There was an old cowboy film on the telly. Ryan watched it with me, on my knee. Well not exactly watched it, but had a packet of crisps and an ice-cream while I was watching it. I spend a lot of time with him since…you know.' Roy paused, to wipe another tear from the corner of his eye. 'He doesn't say but I know he misses him,'

'And?' Monica asked very gently.

'One point when he looked up they were roping steers. This is so fucking stupid - Sorry Mrs O'Leary.' Roy put his hand over his mouth in a gesture of apology.

'I'll tolerate your bad language on this one occasion only. Please try to avoid using those sort of words. What happened next?'

'Well Ryan was really interested in the way they twirled the lassoes and asked me to show him how it was done. So he got off my knee and I took my belt off to try and twirl it and while I was trying to make it go round and round I caught him on his arm. It was an accident, honest Mrs O'Leary. I'd never hurt him on purpose.'

Monica managed not to smile. 'We'll still have to take the kids to the hospital. Let's see if Ryan tells us the same. All he's said so far is that his dad's hit him with a belt. Are you sorted?'

They climbed into Monica's Ford and headed for the nursery first, then the hospital. Ryan was proud to show the doctor his arm with the injury and confirmed that his dad had been showing him how to throw a rope round a cow when it happened.

Monica became the allocated social worker at the child protection conference three weeks later. She was pleased with this, as she was not sure that other workers would recognise the injustice of social work scrutiny brought about by the previous tragic accident to Ricky. If that had never happened, the current incident would have not been seen as so significant.

At three o'clock the following Thursday afternoon, Jake was sitting with Daley in his bedroom in Beech Lodge.

'How do you like it here?'

'You're not going to move me are you?' Daley suddenly looked worried.

Avoiding the question, Jake asked, 'How do you spend your time while you're here?' He'd had reports that

Daley did not really mix with the other young people living there and was anxious to check there was no element of exclusion or racism.

'How are the others who live here? Okay?' Daley thought for a moment and gave a half smile. Whatever he was thinking he wasn't going to share.

Jake started again, 'I'm told you spend a lot of time here, in your room...' Social workers are trained to ask non-leading questions, so as not to suggest answers. Jake was aware he was not doing it well. 'Are there any interests or hobbies you'd like me to see if I can get you set up for? We don't want you getting bored.'

Daley looked across and said, quietly, 'I wouldn't mind some proper oil paints and an easel.'

Jake was surprised. 'I didn't know you were artistic – what sort of things d'you paint?'

Daley responded sharply. 'I haven't been painting – I've not got the things.' And he quietly added, 'Just a bit of drawing.' He reached down to a pile of school-type exercise books and handed the top one to Jake, who opened the first page to find a coloured drawing of his own Peugeot. It had a draughtsman-like detail to it and was, to Jake's eye, of real commercial quality.

'This is amazing. That's my car, right down to the number plate.' Jake turned the pages, to find other vehicles ranging from a BMW R100 chasing a Honda Fireblade to a red Ferrari Marinello. The detail and perspective were perfect on each.

'These are incredible, Daley. Have you done them all in the four weeks you've been here?' Daley nodded.

As Jake turned the pages, entranced, he opened onto a page without motor vehicles. It was a picture of a rose, like the tattoo that he'd seen the night before. The detail was exact and perfect. There was even the same mole drawn next to one of the petals that Jake had caressed and kissed the previous night. There was no question but that it was a picture of Alison's rose. The hairs stood up on the back of Jake's neck as he casually enquired, 'what sort of motor is that?'

Daley paused and blushed a little, 'That was a tattoo I was thinking of having done.' Jake's thoughts went straight back to the last time a foster home had been mentioned to Daley and he had been restrained. Jake remembered blond hair with straggly pink tips and a twelve-year old voice whispering behind him, '… Because he's shagging Alison Bryant.' He'd ignored it at the time because it had seemed so far fetched. He felt cold inside and shuddered.

Turning the page over to reveal Val Kilmer's Batmobile, he said, 'I've found you a foster home.'

Daley said quietly, 'I don't think so.' Then more loudly, 'I don't think so.' And with tears rolling down his cheeks he yelled, 'I'm not fucking going.'

The door burst open and three male workers rushed in. 'Everything alright?'

Jake was shocked at the sudden change in tempo. 'Leave us. We'll be fine,' as Daley pushed past him and the others, through the open bedroom door and ran towards the front door, still crying.

*Internal Memo.*
*To: The Director of Children's Services*
*From: Jacob Atkinson, Social Worker*
*Date 26th July*

<u>Whistleblowing Procedure</u>

*I am the social worker to Daley Andrew Stevens, Accommodated under Section 20, Children Act 1989 and currently resident at Beech Lodge. In the course of my work I have been made aware that Daley Stevens, a fifteen-year-old boy, has been the subject of sexual abuse within Beech Lodge. This came to light as the result of allegations by other residents in the Home. The alleged perpetrator of this abuse is Alison Bryant, Head of Home. The nature of this abuse is sexual intercourse between Ms Bryant and Daley. I have not made formal enquiries into this, but as the result of my own observations believe this to be a well-founded allegation by other children.*
*Jacob Atkinson.*
*Social Worker*

Jake had typed it on his computer at home. It was his fifth draft and it had taken him until 2 in the morning. He had wept while composing it, as he really liked Alison. As he walked through the general office, he dropped the sealed envelope into the internal post tray. It was done.

*The Lord is my Shepherd; I shall not want.*
*He maketh me to lie down in green pastures: He leadeth me beside the still waters.*
*He restoreth my soul: He leadeth me in the paths of righteousness for his name's sake. Yea, though I walk through the valley of the shadow of death, I will fear no evil: for Thou art with me; Thy rod and Thy staff they comfort me.*
*Thou preparest a table before me in the presence of mine enemies: Thou anointest my head with oil; my cup runneth over.*
*Surely goodness and mercy shall follow me all the days of my life: and I will dwell in the house of the Lord for ever.*

The words of the twenty-third psalm were running through Christine McBride's head as she walked home from church on Sunday night. It was seven-thirty in the evening and a bit chilly. The twenty-third was Chrissie's favourite. She thought of it often as she walked through the Valley of the Shadow of Death. Sometimes it was a visit to Thorpe Park Estate. Tonight she knew she had to walk past the rowdy nightclub on Parsons Street. She considered it was a particularly disgusting one. It was frequented by homosexuals, lesbians and drug users.

The Vicar's sermon had been quite touching this evening. He had spoken of the need for tolerance and the importance of living in harmony with those of different races and faiths. He was absolutely right, of course. Christine was scrupulous in her work not to show prejudice and had worked side-by-side in the Royal Air Force with a Jewish girl, two black girls and several non-believers as well as the normal ones like herself. They were all nice enough and if they didn't do their jobs properly, it was nothing to do with race or faith. She still wasn't comfortable however, with nightclub-goers and wasn't sure about Muslims.

As she approached DV8 nightclub, she crossed the road. *Yea though I walk through the valley of the shadow of death, I will fear no evil: for thou art with me; thy rod and thy staff they comfort me.* She stopped, as she saw Sally Beckett on the opposite pavement, walking towards her with a friend, a nice-looking young woman in a flowing skirt. She was about to call out a cheery good evening, but thought better of it. She was by now opposite that nightclub and she certainly didn't want a response from anyone else in its vicinity; so she stopped and waited for Sally to glance across and come over the road to have a chat. She felt warm towards Sally. Sally was the one colleague in the team who was not standoffish to her and if ever she had to jointly visit anyone, she would always prefer to go with Sally.

As she waited, Sally did not look across the road. Chrissie watched with some surprise as she walked through the doors of the nightclub with her friend. Chrissie wondered if she hadn't met the friend before. She was vaguely familiar. Chrissie's surprise at seeing them walk into that club turned to shock as she clearly saw Sally in the lobby slip her hand into the other girl's as they walked through the inner doors out of sight.

Chrissie decided as she walked back to her flat that it must be necessary to pretend to be a couple if you were going into such a place, although why anyone would want to go there if they were normal and sane was something Christine McBride could not work out. Perhaps Sally was doing some research. Or something.

Then she remembered where she had met the other girl. Her name was Geraldine. She had been introduced to her by Jake Atkinson when he first started at the office. There had been an office party where partners were invited and she had been Jake's partner. She had been introduced to Sally at the same time and as Chrissie recalled, had spent a lot of time that evening quietly talking to Sally. They had seemed to really hit it off. It had only been a few days after that when she'd asked Jake how Geraldine was and he said they'd split up. She suddenly went cold. She recalled that she'd asked Jake if Geraldine had gone off with another feller and Jake had replied that she'd shacked up with a woman. A lesbian called Sylvia. Gone to the dark side, Monica had called it and she'd made some vulgar comment about a bird in the hand and two in each other's bush. Surely Sally wasn't one of them?

Christine poured herself a stiff whisky and put it into a glass of hot milk when she got home and went straight to bed.

Monday morning in the office. Chrissie and Sally were at their desks, when Chrissie's curiosity got the better of her. She had to know.

'Good weekend?'

Sally looked up from her file notes. 'Not bad, thanks Chrissie. Spent loads of time in the new D-I-Y superstore. We're installing a new bedroom at home and Gerry's building one in, so we were getting everything flatpacked.'

'Gerry a carpenter, then?' Christine's heart sank as Sally used the name. It might be.

'No, Gerry's my partner and we're both novices to any sort of do-it yourself. But between us, we'll get it done. We've been sleeping in a makeshift bedroom for ages, so it'll be good to have it done.'

Christine took the information in. Five minutes passed as they both went back to writing.

They were interrupted by Frances. 'Ah, the dynamic duo. Could the pair of you do a little job for me? I've got a call from a school about a child called Samuel Abraham. Seven years old. Apparently he's got a bizarre pattern of bruising on his back. Sort of interlinked, almost diagonal hearts. The teacher who rang described it as looking like Minuets. It's Thorpe Park again. The Police can't spare anyone at the moment, so would the pair of you mind doing it jointly, as the school describes the mother as odd.'

'Could that have been Minarets?' Sally looked up.

'Could have been. Anyway, as soon as you can.' She handed a referral form to Sally, who briefly read it. With it was a faxed simplistic drawing of a geometric pattern. It looked slightly like the spires on the Kremlin from an unusual angle.

Chrissie and Sally swung into a well-practised routine. While Sally telephoned the Child Protection Register to see if he was known, Chrissie assembled the necessary forms to be filled in. Ten minutes later, they were in Sally's car on the way to Thorpe Park.

No doorbell, but a knocker on the door. A surprisingly heavy one. Standing on the doorstep, they both eyed the door with some trepidation.

'It looks like the kind of door that would be answered by Vlad the Impaler with a knocker like that,' Sally whispered with a smile on her face.

Christine was in a pensive mood. *I shall fear no evil,* as Sally lifted the large iron ball and let it drop once against the door.

It was a big, fierce-looking white woman with red cheeks who opened the door. Very big, both in height and width. She appeared to be in her late thirties or early forties and had her hair piled and wound on top of her head like a cottage loaf. Her pinafore was fierce as well, giving the 'strictly work' message. She held a poker in her hand in the way a policeman holds a truncheon. Chrissie opened her mouth to introduce herself and Sally, but no sound came out. *Vlad the Impaler.* Sally stepped in.

'Ms Abraham? May we come in? We're from Children's Services and it's about Samuel.' She took out her identity card, which was closely and silently inspected by Rebecca Abraham, who stepped back without a word to let the pair of social workers in.

They were ushered into the most unusual front room either had ever seen. In the middle of it was a low table which looked as if it had been fashioned with an axe. The only item on it was a huge black leather-bound book. The walls were stark white, with two bookshelves, which were in the same style as the table. What struck Chrissie most was that apart from the light on the ceiling, a bare bulb, there was nothing electrical or vaguely modern in the room at all. The wooden floorboards looked well-scrubbed and there was a rug of the type made by threading wool through netting. They were silently offered a hard wooden chair each to sit on. Sally, briefly worried about laddering her tights, paused before she sat.

Rebecca Abraham, still silent, stood over them and at last opened her mouth.

'Well?' Her voice was as deep as any woman's voice could be.

'Ms Abraham, we're social workers. I'm sorry, but we've had a report from Samuel's school that he has been observed to have an unusual pattern of bruising on his back. We've an obligation to investigate any unexplained injury to a child under Section 47 of the Children Act.' Rebecca Abraham said nothing.

'The 1989 Children Act.' Sally was stalling while she gathered her thoughts, then went on, 'We have a set of procedures to follow and have to make sure children are safe.' She paused and smiled politely and expectantly hoping for a response from this scary woman. Nothing came forth. Sally, relieved, observed that she was no longer carrying the poker.

'Apparently the pattern is one of interlinked inverted minarets.' Rebecca Abraham looked puzzled. 'Not unlike upside-down onions joined up.'

Without a word, Rebecca Abraham shuffled out of the room, returning a short while later, carrying something. She spoke.

'Something like that?' In her hand was a carpet beater, its wire frame neatly woven in inverted heart shapes.

'We have, as I said, to follow procedures,' began Sally, when she was interrupted.

'Procedures. I'll tell you about procedures.' Rebecca was clearly upset. Her face had turned red and as she spoke, she had harp strings between her top and bottom teeth. She picked up the huge leather volume from the table and slammed it down on the table, making the room shake.

'These are my procedures. The Holy Bible is the word of the Lord. The Bible tells us: He who spareth the rod hateth his son: but he that loveth him correcteth him betimes. That's Proverbs 13:24. Withhold not correction from a child: for if thou strike him with the rod, he shall not die. Thou shalt beat him with the rod and deliver his soul from hell. That's Proverbs 23:13 to 14.' As she delivered the message, her voice rose and she emphasised loudly Deliver His Soul From Hell. 'My procedures are the word of the Lord and no do-gooding heathens will turn me from the paths of righteousness.'

At this point Chrissie found her voice. She was angry at the misuse of the Holy word. 'Ms Abraham, you have not the right to break the law and abuse your child. There are some issues in which you may believe, but you are subject to the law of the land if you choose to live here. It is child abuse to inflict an injury on your son, whatever your beliefs. We have an obligation to investigate procedurally and if necessary report it to the Police, which we will be doing. Now what I need from you is an absolute assurance that you will not be punishing Samuel in such a way as to injure him in the future. Ever. If you can't give us that absolute promise, we will have to consider removal of the child.'

Rebecca Abraham stood stock-still for two minutes at least before responding. She spoke quietly when she did.

'I've no choice. I will have to do what you want.'

'How can we be sure you will?' Chrissie was quick in answering.

Rebecca put her hand on the Bible, closed her eyes and tilted her head towards the ceiling. 'I swear on the Holy Bible that I will not injure Samuel through punishment in the future.' She opened her eyes again and looked first at Christine then at Sally. 'Is that good enough?'

'I think I can speak for my colleague in saying that we are prepared to accept your promise at this time. However, I have to advise you that you are likely to receive a visit from the Police and one of us will be back in a few days to undertake what we call a core assessment. There is also likely to be a Child Protection Conference, which I would guess will result in a care plan and several future visits from social workers in the coming months. Are you prepared to accept that?'

'If it's the Lord's will, so be it.' Rebecca sat down at last.

Sally resumed, taking details of the family. She established that in the immediate family there were only Rebecca and Samuel and noted down history, dates of birth and more distant relatives. A half hour later they got up to leave.

Both were quiet as Sally drove back to the office. Sally was wondering how Samuel Abraham had escaped the notice of social workers to date. Christine was still wondering whether it was possible Sally could really be a lesbian. As Sally turned the car out of Thorpe Park, Christine was considering ways of asking whether Sally's relationship with Geraldine was indeed an unholy one.

'There is something I've always wondered. I hope you don't mind me asking, but is Sally a shortened version of anything? It's just my niece is expecting and we think it's going to be a girl. The whole family's been asked to think up possible names and without wanting to be too personal, I think your name's lovely.'

Sally hesitated. 'I believe it's a derivative of Sarah, but my real name's Sylvia, which I've always thought just wasn't me, so I've been Sally since I was about sixteen. Very few people call me Sylvia. Gerry does and my mum does when she's angry. The only reason Gerry calls me Sylvia as opposed to Sally is because of a love of Thunderbirds, created of course by Gerry and Sylvia Anderson.'

Chrissie took the information in. She noted that Sally never referred to Gerry as He or She. *And I'll bet you see yourselves as a pair of Thunderbirds in a different context.* She gave a cold smile and stared forward through the windscreen. Now she hated Sally.

Five weeks later to the day, Rebecca Abraham was convicted of Assault Occasioning Actual Bodily Harm. She was unrepresented in court and pleaded guilty. As good as her word, she never injured Samuel again.

'Can you cope for an hour or so?' Alison Bryant looked across at Craig, her deputy. 'It's just that I've been called to go and see Hilary Campbell.'

'The boss? What does she want to see you about?' Craig was more curious than concerned. 'She doesn't normally give us the time of day and I can't remember when I last saw her down here at the Unit.'

Craig and Alison were quite close. Between them they had been in charge of Beech Lodge for four years, with Alison as the manager and Craig as the deputy manager. If they were on duty together, they would sometimes go off quietly to one of the night-staff bedrooms and enjoy a quiet hour or so having sex. As far as the resident children were concerned, it was a meeting or they were doing paperwork. As all the young people were at school, it was a good time and that is precisely what they had been doing. Craig was married with two small children and a stay-at-home wife. She hadn't suspected anything during the four years and would never find out. Both Craig and Alison regarded it as a casual affair. They had made an agreement between them not to get possessive, committed or jealous about each other and not to ask about other relationships. As far as Craig knew, Alison was not spreading herself about anyway, so there would be no chance of a sexually transmitted infection for him to take home. Alison was fun. She would experiment sexually and have a go at anything. It was perfect, as far as Craig was concerned. From Alison's point of view, she was happy with the arrangement. She regarded herself as highly sexed and had her physical needs met by Craig whenever she wanted. She never told him if she had any sort of relationship with anyone else and let him believe, quite wrongly, that he was the only man she had sex with. He was, after all, the only member of her staff that she had sex with, so he wasn't too far wrong.

'It's probably to tell us that now we're up to quota on children that we've got to take an extra one or two for the Emergency Duty Team on a crisis basis if they ask. That's what she usually does.' Alison, although unconcerned about the request, did wonder why it could not wait for supervision.

It was a week since her evening with Jake. She rather liked Jake and appreciated his sense of humour. Also the fact that he could cook. He was quite classy as well and didn't mind paying for the drinks.

'See you in an hour or so, Craig,' she called as she closed the front door.

At three-thirty precisely she knocked on the door of Hilary's office.

'Come in.' Hilary was sitting behind her desk for a change rather than in one of the softer chairs. Next to her, almost behind the desk was a man Alison did not know.

'Alison, this is Graham Percival from Human Resources. Please take a seat.'

Alison was surprised to see someone else in the office. Both Hilary and Graham appeared uncomfortable.

'Alison, I have a difficult and rather embarrassing situation on my hands which I have to share with you,' Hilary began. 'I've received an allegation from a member of staff to the effect that your treatment of one of the young people in Beech Lodge has been unprofessional. Now I know that this is a position that residential workers find themselves in all too often and I must stress that I and the Authority have the utmost faith in you. To be entirely honest, I'm not happy about the letter I've received and in confidence I'm not sure that I fully trust the member of staff concerned. The young person named is Daley Stevens, the new resident.' Hilary paused and took a deep breath.

'So I presume you're going to suspend me?' To Hilary's surprise Alison was calm and looked entirely at ease with the situation.

'Unfortunately we have no option but to do so. However, you have my word that we will get this cleared up as quickly as possible with a view to getting you back into work. You're probably aware that you can't contact anyone from work, are not allowed on work premises, will be paid your full salary and are not considered guilty of anything. I will be in touch with you by telephone on at least a weekly basis. Is there anything you would like to say?'

Alison glanced at Hilary's desk while Hilary was speaking and saw the letter Hilary was looking at as she spoke. Having noted Jake Atkinson's name at the bottom of it, she responded.

'This is difficult for me. I don't have any problem with an allegation or indeed being suspended while any such allegation is investigated. You haven't told me who has contacted you and I'm not asking. The children are the most important thing and if there is any question that one of them may not have been properly cared for, I would much rather it be fully investigated so everyone is assured they are treated as well as they can possibly be. As far as I am aware, there is nothing I have done and nothing I would intentionally ever do which might prevent my kids getting the best I and my staff can offer. And they are my kids.' Alison paused and smiled as a tear ran down her cheek. She continued, 'As long as it's not Jacob Atkinson that's made the allegation.'

Both Hilary and Graham sat up in their seats.

'What prompts you to say that?' Hilary had tried to ask the question in a measured way so as to avoid suggesting that it was indeed Jake.

'This is the most difficult bit for me,' Alison looked down. 'I was going to telephone and ask to come and see you this afternoon about an entirely different issue to do with him.'

'Go on.' Hilary had no idea where Alison was going with this.

'Yesterday evening,' Alison paused, looked down and started to sob. 'A couple of nights ago he…' Louder sobs. 'He raped me.' Floods of tears followed, as Hilary moved out from behind the desk to offer tissues and put her arm round Alison.

'I know it's difficult, but can you tell me the circumstances or any more about it?'

Between the tears, Alison wiped her nose on her sleeve and several minutes later was able to stammer between sobs, 'He saw me when he was out running and I was walking home, bumped into me and invited me out for a drink. I accepted and he got me really drunk then took me back to his flat. It was there that he…' Alison was in floods of tears again.

'You don't have to tell us any more. I need you to go and report it to the police. As it's so recent they may be able to get forensic evidence. I'll call them now.'

'I need to go home and put some make-up on. I can't see them looking like this.' Alison was a quick thinker. Whose DNA would they find if they did forensic tests?

'I'll go straight to the police after that.'

Are you sure you'll be okay?' Hilary was concerned and angry. Obviously Atkinson had thought he could cover his own appalling actions by discrediting this unfortunate woman he had abused. She'd suspend him immediately.

'I'll manage. Thanks, Hilary. I won't be reporting for work until I've heard from you, then.' Alison gathered up her things and left.

Jake thought he would be contacted two or three working days after sending the memo. It was on a Monday over a week later that Frances walked to his desk, with an exceptionally red face.

'Come into my office. Now.' Her mouth was set and pursed like a bulldog's bottom. As he followed her in, she said, 'Don't bother to sit down. You're in big trouble.'

'Go on,' Jake responded.

'I have on my desk two allegations. The first is from you alleging there has been sexual abuse in Beech Lodge. The second and far more serious one contains the fact that you are guilty of the rape of a colleague. As the result of that, you are suspended from duty. You are to leave this office, without speaking to anyone. You are not to contact anyone from the office or discuss it with any member of staff. There will be an enquiry. I…' and Jake thought he could see a half smile, '…am obliged to notify the Police and the General Social Care Council.'

Jake was surprised, angry, upset and confused. He turned without a word, collected his leather jacket and left the office by the back door. And Do Not Pass Go. Do

Not Collect Two Hundred Pounds. Hell hath no fury like a woman spermed.

'As the result of matters I can't devolve, I've to reallocate a number of cases.' Frances seemed in an exceptionally jolly mood during the team meeting. 'I've got a blue baby and two young offenders.'

'What colour? If it's anything like jelly babies, I like the green ones.' Tom chuckled at his own joke. The team joined in.

'Monnie does too – you Irish are all the same,' Chrissie retorted.

Monica spun round, a look of anger on her face, 'As long as you don't have to have the black ones, I suppose.'

There was a hushed silence and Frances stepped in with, 'Jelly babies are nice, I like the orange ones and it's such a nice change to have a joke in the team. Christine, you'll deal with Harley Moss. He's the blue baby. Mother will need a lot of support. Monica, I'd like you to see to Daley Stevens. He's at Beech Lodge and shouldn't pose too many problems. Sally, I'm afraid I'll have to ask you to deal with Curtis Wilson. He's coloured and a troublemaker.'

Curtis heard the G4S van come to a halt. He had been inside it, sitting in a tiny enclosed space on his own for over two hours, and had vomited twice and wet himself once. It was not an unusual occurrence in Group 4 Securicor secure transport.

It was three weeks since his first court appearance, and he'd spent those three weeks in secure accommodation, remanded while a Social Enquiry report was done by a woman he'd never met before. He hated secure accommodation. He'd heard nothing from Jake, his social worker, who he liked and trusted. Now he was going to Young Offenders Institution, and was terrified.

'Welcome to Wetherby Holiday Camp. I'll give you some helpful advice – don't try playing them up.'

Curtis had been found guilty of assaulting a security guard with a weapon at the supermarket, having chosen the wrong direction in which to run when the Police arrived, and having refused to name his friends who had got away. He knew it was untrue, and pointed out that the knife they showed him was still wrapped in its supermarket wrapping. The fact that he'd never set eyes on it before was not believed by either the Police or the Magistrates. Now, facing twelve months in Young Offenders Institution, he was extremely frightened. His fear was not only for himself, but for his mother, as he was sure she would not cope without him, and he thought they might put her in hospital.

He was ushered out of the van, and found himself in an enclosed yard with high doors behind him. He was ushered through the entrance to find a reception counter with a man in uniform behind it.

'Clothes off, and put them on the counter. Are you carrying any weapons drugs or cigarettes?'

Too nervous to speak, Curtis tried desperately not to wee again and shook his head.

'Now your clothes are removed, you will do ten star jumps. The purpose of this is to establish you are not attempting to conceal anything on your body.'

Curtis complied. A strip search was something new to Curtis.

'This is yours.' Bedroll, navy blue sweat shirt marked WBY on the front, green stiff trousers missing the top button, socks and shoes. 'You wear your own underpants and can have them brought in. We will inspect them for contraband before they are given to you. We can't allow you a belt or laces, but if you earn enough privileges, you will be able to have trainers.'

His allotted clothing fitted his skinny frame quite reasonably, and the rules he was given seemed bearable. He guessed that for himself, he was going to cope with his time inside. He wouldn't have guessed that he would be better fed there than he had been in the whole of his life.

At home, from a very early age, he had taken to discreetly searching the neighbours' bins to see what was in there that he could eat. He was scrupulous about taking whatever he found home and washing it in the sink before eating it. Sometimes he would put it in the microwave to warm it up. Once he reached the age of eight, he dared not tell anyone he fed himself this way, for fear he would be laughed at by his friends.

His mother, Dolly would sometimes imagine she saw things, and sometimes would have conversations with people who weren't there. She also had conversations with God. What she didn't do was run an ordered home. Curtis' job was to make sure she got by every day. Sometimes it would be putting her clothes out for her, sometimes walking her to the shops, always seeing the television was on, and taking her to the church on a Sunday. That way, at least she wouldn't get the Authorities threatening to take her into hospital and him into Care. When he had to deal with social workers, he spoke in his best accent, and made sure he had clothes that were clean. He was used to the launderette, but could wash clothes in the bath if he had to. Social workers would generally believe he and Dolly were coping, and close the case until the next crisis.

Sitting in his new accommodation, he thought: '…as long as I keep my nose clean…', and a tear ran down one of his cheeks. He loved Dolly, as only a son can love his mum, and knew he wouldn't see her for at least a few months.


It was 11 o'clock on a Saturday morning in early July and Jake didn't want to get out of bed. He'd been in bed most of the week following his suspension. The door bell was ringing, for the fourth time. Whoever it was wasn't going to go away. Jake eased himself out of bed and slipped on a pair of joggers and a black T-shirt. He was surprised when he opened his door to find Monnie standing there.

'Well, are y'inviting me in or what, lazy fecker?'

'Sorry, come in and I'll put the kettle on.' Jake had a week's growth of beard and hadn't brushed his hair.

'You can wash your bloody hands first. Did I get you out of bed?'

'No, I had to get up for the doorbell.'

Monnie smiled and, following Jake into the kitchen, perched on one of the kitchen stools while Jake waited for the kettle to boil. 'Now then, Jake what's happened?'

Jake shifted uncomfortably, 'I'm not allowed to discuss it.'

Monnie focused her sharp grey eyes on Jake's face and a knowing smile appeared. 'I suspected it was a suspension. What's it for?'

Jake paused to put two scoops of Lavazza Black in the cafetiere and half filled it. 'Milk and sugar?'

'I like my coffee the same as I like my men. Smooth dark and rich. I'll have a black one today,' she chortled.

Jake handed her a cup of black coffee and said coldly, 'To answer your question, there's a letter on the fridge. I'm accused of raping a colleague.'

Monnie coughed with surprise, spitting her coffee across the kitchen. 'Fecking shite, you're kidding.'

There was a long pause as Jake sipped at his coffee. 'I wish.'

Monnie appeared to have trouble getting her breath. 'Who, how, when? It's not your style – my perv antennae would have known. What are you willing to tell me?'

So Jake recounted the whole tale, of the run, knocking Alison over, the pub, the night they spent together, the pubic rose, Daley's drawing, the pink tips and the whistleblowing letter.

Monica was furious, 'That Alison Bryant's a cunt. She'll not get away with it.'

Jake felt a lump coming in his throat, 'So you believe me?'

'I'll see the drawing. Course I do.' Monica got off her stool and crossed the kitchen to reach up and put her arms around Jake.

As Jake sobbed silently, Monica whispered, 'I've an idea.'

# Six

Christine McBride was feeling exceptionally morose. Ever since she had found out Sally's relationship was perverse, she had not been able to bring herself to speak to her. It had always been the same; as soon as you thought you had a friend, you lost her, you got moved or she went off you.

Christine had been born in Crieff, not far from Perth in Scotland. She was the only child of Alice McBride, who'd conceived her whilst drunk. Alice had not been a high-flyer. She had a drink problem and couldn't look after herself, let alone a baby as well in the early 1950s. Perhaps fortunately, Alice had five sisters. From a very early age, Chrissie consequently had six mothers, most of whom were much more interested in their own children than they were in Alice's bastard offspring. They were also spread out between Glasgow and Dundee and so

Chrissie changed families and schools every few months for most of her life.

At seventeen, she managed to get into the Royal Air Force. They made sure she had a clean, crisp uniform and shiny shoes. They made sure she had food in her tummy and a bed to sleep in that she knew was hers. They told her what the rules were and she loved every minute of it. She never became really friendly with the others in the RAF and wasn't particularly interested in boys. She'd found as a child that if she went to Sunday school and was interested in the Bible, that she would get more love and attention than she ever got at home. It was a habit that never left her and she had grown to love the Holy Scriptures, reading them for hours while her colleagues put on makeup and went out on dates.

On leaving the Air Force, she found a job as an administrative assistant in a local government social services office. She had moved from office work to being a social work assistant until she gained a place on a qualification course to become a social worker. She was conscious of Luke Chapter 18 Verse 16 in the work: *But Jesus called them unto him and said, Suffer little children to come unto me and forbid them not: for of such is the kingdom of God.* She hoped and hinted to her clients that she could be a Godmother to children on her caseload. And so it came to pass.

Christine was so disappointed with Sally. She had been the nearest thing to a friend that she had, but she could not get out of her mind Jude Chapter 1 Verse 7: *Even as Sodom and Gomorrha and the cities about them in like manner, giving themselves over to fornication and going after strange flesh, are set forth for an example, suffering the vengeance of eternal fire.* Sally was going after strange flesh and would without question suffer the vengeance of eternal fire. Corinthians Chapter 6 Verse 9 made it clear: *Know ye not that the unrighteous shall not inherit the kingdom of God? Be not deceived: neither fornicators, nor idolaters, nor adulterers, nor effeminate, nor abusers of themselves with mankind...* It's true that is about male homosexuality, but Chrissie had discussed it with the vicar and was assured that female homosexuality was every bit as unholy. How could Sally do the Lord's work and be leading the sort of life she was? Chrissie decided to let the Lord guide her. Presumably she would be shown the way forward in the fullness of time.

'Lakhi, my love, stay right there.'

Lakshmi was lying on her bed with her lover Naren, wondering about the future. Naren sat up, reached over to his jacket pocket and took out a Pentax Optio camera. Walking round the bed dressed only in boxer shorts, he had taken four or five pictures before she realised what he was doing.

'Stop it. Stop it. I've got no clothes on. Why are you taking pictures?'

'My lovely Lakhi, it's what people in love do. I will remind myself of your beauty when we are not together and that way you can always be with me at your most beautiful.' Lakshmi was not convinced. Why have a photograph when the real thing is available? He had repeatedly told her she needed to be less inhibited. Lakshmi did not think of herself as knowledgeable in the language of love. Her marriage had been arranged when she was still a teenager and had lasted just over ten years until her husband had run off with another woman, leaving her with a small baby. She reluctantly let Naren take his pictures and made a mental note to ask her sister Puja whether it was normal.

The day hadn't started too badly for Lakshmi Patel. She had a new boyfriend in her life, Naren Bhargava, whom she had met through the internet dating site, Hindu Match. She was secretly embarrassed about her use of the internet in this way, but it had yielded a result. Until now, it had seemed like a good result. Naren was a stocky five foot eight and fifty one years old, even featured with an impressive moustache. A brown spot on his nose, but it merely emphasised for Lakshmi his other noble features. Naren was coming round to see her, bringing a recent Bollywood movie and she had prepared Moti Chur Laddu, a North Indian sweet dish for happy occasions. She had known Naren now for six weeks and while the other members of her family disliked him, it really did not matter to her. He was mean with money and Lakshmi had to pay whenever they went out, but he had mentioned the possibility of marriage and said he owned six properties, so he must be a good prospect financially. He wanted to become part of their family unit and asked many times for Lakshmi to change her will so he could be executor should it become necessary and personally make sure Nikhil, Lakshmi's son would be well looked after. She had not been and was still not sure about that.

What had been a real mystery to Lakshmi was the depth of Naren's knowledge about her personal circumstances. On the day she had had a short conversation with Jake Atkinson at work, she had been approached as she was leaving to go home by Frances Phillips and Frances' manager, Hilary Campbell. They had taken her back into Frances' office, told her the Audit Department was investigating her and informed her she had to be suspended pending the outcome of the investigation. She had been allowed to collect her personal possessions from her desk and had been escorted out. That had been a fortnight prior. Naren had told her they were going to do that and that she would be visited within the week by two Audit Investigators, which she was. He had even known that the Audit Investigators, John and Chas would come back and visit her yesterday. They had asked about all sorts of things that she didn't think could be anything to do with the Council – her previous lodgers, how she raised the deposit for her house, how she paid Nikhil's private school fees and about any work she did outside of her social work job. Naren had said that she would be seen to have broken the law. She had underpaid her Council tax while she had lodgers, had hidden money from the Department for Work and Pensions which she used for the deposit on her house while on Benefits and had as one of her lodgers an illegal immigrant (or as Naren described it, an Illegal living with you). As a result, Lakshmi was terrified she may go to prison. Naren comforted her, telling her that he would be able to stop the investigation. All she needed to do was wait and let it be passed to the police and then he would tell her what to say. He would take care of the rest and he could. He had important and influential connections.

Naren put down the camera. 'I have an important matter to discuss with you Lakhi. You need to take action to be sure your will properly offers care and security for Nikhil should anything happen to you. Make me the executor of your will and I will guarantee that should it become necessary he will have nothing but the best. There is of course no financial advantage to me, but it is entirely out of love for you and Nikhil that I will give freely of my legal expertise.'

It was a suggestion he had made several times before. She was not prepared to commit herself to this at least until the relationship was more established.

'Why do you keep asking this? If there is no advantage for you why do you repeatedly request it?' It was a curiosity question more than anything else, so she was surprised at the response this question prompted.

'Bitch. What are you suggesting? I am offering to do you a favour and you accuse me of dishonesty.'

'It wouldn't be a favour to me. I'd be dead if it needed to take effect.' It was intended to be light hearted, but Lakshmi thought for a minute that Naren was going to hit her. Retaining her composure and masking her fear, she said, 'I think you'd better leave now.'

Naren put his clothes back on. As he left, he hissed, 'You could live to regret this disobedience.'

The Moti Chur Laddu did not get eaten. Lakshmi was left with an uneasy feeling that the photographs might come back to haunt her.

Frances Phillips was sitting in her office; she put down her copy of Community Care where she had been checking how much they were paying to Team Managers in other Authorities. It was almost time for her to move on. Frances had a habit of staying in one place for no more than two or three years and she'd done twenty-six months so far in her present place. The job was not an easy one and it was not going easily. She had a relatively new temporary worker, Jake Atkinson. Jake was, like most men, arrogant and aggressive and full of self confidence. She didn't like him, but then, she didn't particularly like men. Social work is predominantly a woman's profession. Men will never understand that the real abuse perpetrated in society is by men on women and all the other stuff pales into insignificance alongside that. She'd been fortunate in a roundabout way, to have the opportunity to suspend him. The difficulty with that was she now had two members of her team suspended. Jacob's suspension she considered was of her own making, whereas Lakshmi's was not. Lakshmi was an extremely good worker. She was dedicated, her records were up to date and she was popular with service users. Of course having an Indian woman in the team also did a lot for a team manager's street cred. It would go on her CV when she wrote her next application that she had supervised ethnic staff.

Francis had been phoned by Hilary Campbell, her Manager and Hilary had said that she had a very difficult situation on her hands and that she would need to deal with it TODAY…She was coming down.

In Frances' office Hilary made sure that Frances understood they had no choice. They had to suspend Lakshmi. It had come from higher up. Lakshmi was being subjected to an Audit Investigation for apparently quite serious fraud both in and outside work but predominantly outside. Frances had been surprised and recognised she had no choice but to attend and watch as Lakshmi accepted what was said and left with dignity.

Frances had some sympathy and felt compassion for Lakshmi. She didn't know what Lakshmi might have done and couldn't imagine that she would have done anything to upset people in the Council. But a Management Instruction is a Management Instruction. She had to comply. Lakshmi Patel's difficulties were probably the result of the actions of some man, she considered on reflection. Lakshmi didn't give a lot away.

Frances had a pen picture of Lakshmi married to a University Lecturer or Doctor and living in one of those middle-class comfortable areas up by the University. She was certainly too refined to belong to a corner shop family and, as far as Frances was concerned, lecturing, medicine and running a corner shop were about the only occupations Asian families had.

Suspension. She had two major concerns. The first was how she was to reallocate the work. Her team weren't busy like she'd seen in other areas, although most of them complained about how much they were doing and the growing level of paperwork. There was no chance, according to Hilary Campbell, of agency replacements while two of them were suspended, as their salary costs still had to be met. The other worry was about whose budget any extra costs would come out of.

Frances' budgetary control was only over funds to basically keep children from coming to risk of serious harm. They called it Section 17 money, as that was the part of the Children Act from which it came. Some families knew just how to use the system and used Section 17 as a second income. Frances didn't really care how the money was used. She took the yearly budget of

£15,000, divided it by twelve and made sure she didn't authorise more than that per month, so as to neither overspend nor underspend. The measure of a good manager nowadays. Her team was not a bad one. Tom was sound enough in his social work practice, although the union stuff he did was a minor irritation. Still, better to have control of him and his trade union activity than not. He was intimidated by her and she knew he would never challenge her, although he called it Respect. Sally was a Gem. Reliable, responsible and professionally turned out. Chrissie was solid and she had a lot of experience. It was true, on reflection, that some of her practice was old-fashioned and that she shouldn't really take up the responsibilities of being a Godparent to children on her caseload. However, Chrissie was Chrissie and you accepted it. Monica needed to be watched. Bright, potentially undermining, but you couldn't help but like her. And the public did as well. She'd got the team out of many a scrape with difficult punters. The positives outweighed the negatives. And then there was Lakshmi and Jacob. Her absent reserves. Lakshmi would surely be back soon. Frances hadn't really got to know her in her two years there. She didn't speak about herself and Frances hadn't asked. She got on with her work, quietly and reliably. She couldn't give Lakshmi a Court report to do, as her written English was probably not really up to it. She'd heard Lakshmi take a call and speak in Indian. Frances thought the Gujerati she spoke was probably Bengali or Urdu. Whatever. She didn't cause any problems and was punctual and reliable. As for Jacob, if Jacob was dismissed, she'd get a female replacement. Pity, really, because he was a not bad social worker and she'd given him all those cases her other team members wouldn't want and he'd just got on with them. Maybe next time she'd get another ethnic one, to help move her up the ladder in her next role.

As she glanced down, she saw a Service Manager post advertised in Peterborough, with experience of supervising black and ethnic minority staff as a desirable attribute. Her attention was back in the pages of Community Care.

The day after the incident with the camera, Naren visited again. He came round as if nothing had happened the day before.

He sat with Lakshmi and said, 'You know I really love you; I think you're the best woman I've ever found and when we get married we will send Nikhil to Eton College and perhaps we will go to India. Incidentally while we're on the subject of Nikhil, you need to make me the Executor on your will. I've got legal knowledge and contacts and if anything should happen, we need to make sure he's absolutely properly looked after.' He whispered seductively to her in Hindi, 'Mei tumse pyar karpa hui.'

She answered also in Hindi that she loved him too, 'Mei aapse pyar karpi hui.' Somehow, Hindi, the language of love, made it feel like the seal on an intimate bond. He poured them both a glass of Chianti Classico wine from a bottle he had brought and they toasted their future. Lakshmi may have had some minor niggling doubts about Naren but said nothing. She did not know whether she could spend her life with a man who didn't seem interested in the dignity and honour of her shrine and she was not even sure whether Naren loved the Lord Krishna, to whom she often prayed. Naren had told Lakshmi that although he was married his marriage was fast coming to an end and no sooner had he got his divorce through then he would declare to the world his undying love in marrying Lakshmi and they would be together.

Aware of how tight Naren was with his money Lakshmi was surprised when he went to his car and brought out for her a large bunch of flowers which he gave to her. They were red roses and yellow carnations. She smiled and expressed her appreciation and she said she would place them by the shrine where they could serve a dual purpose of beauty and commitment to her God.

As she went to the kitchen to cut the base off the flower stalks Naren said, 'Would you very much mind if I checked my e-mails on your computer?'

'Of course not,' was Lakshmi's automatic response and she left him in the second reception room doing just that.

Having placed the flowers she came back into the room with Naren and he looked at her, 'I'm sorry,' he said, 'I have an apology to make.'

She said, 'Yes?' her heart racing, expecting him to speak about the events of yesterday, with such love and commitment as to make amends.

To her surprise, he continued, 'I've had to take a thousand pounds from your money drawer to cover my expenses. I've spent an awful lot of money wining and dining people from the Audit Department and buying them tickets for Alton Towers for their family. It's cost me a thousand pounds, so I've taken it back.' Lakshmi was initially disappointed, shocked and not particularly happy with it. However, Naren had promised to marry her and if it was to happen it had be something that she must learn to accept.

Lakshmi had a habit of putting money and change into a money drawer in the study. She did this in order to use it whenever Nikhil wanted new trainers or anything else such as school books, pencils, pens or money to go to the cinema. She would also use it to take money to the temple where she would always put it into the offerings container. She had not been aware that Naren even knew of the existence of the drawer and had been taken aback when he had taken some money out of it. It had contained somewhere between four and six thousand pounds and a thousand pounds taken from it was not an insignificant amount.

Lakshmi looked at Naren, 'Why?' she asked. And to clarify her question, 'Why would you need to wine and dine people from the Audit department? Why would you need to buy them tickets for anything?'

Naren smiled and said, 'Don't worry about it Lakhi. I've got it all under control. I will make sure they do what is best for you. When the time comes I will get them to do exactly what is needed provided you follow my instructions.'

He reached across and kissed her, sliding his hand down her arm and on to her stomach over her clothes. Nikhil was at school and a longing to be held and loved helped her put behind her the events of the previous day. They went upstairs.

Shortly before Nikhil came home from school, Lakshmi felt strange. She was dizzy and felt sick. Naren had left and she had been pondering the recent events. Seized by an urge to vomit, she rushed to the bathroom. As she came from the bathroom, she headed for the bedroom to lie down and could not be sure when she woke later sideways on her bed whether she had fainted or fallen asleep immediately.

She woke with a headache to find Nikhil, her A-Star student prince standing over her anxiously and got up to cook for him. As she served him, she decided she needed the toilet. Again.

Two weeks after Sarah and Harley's visit to Dr Gohil, Harley Moss was still in hospital. He'd been admitted as a result of one of his fits, which had happened in a hospital outpatient room while he was due to be seen by Dr Gohil. They'd kept him in hospital for further tests and encouraged Sarah Moss to visit as frequently as she possibly could. She visited daily, looking at the baby and cooing over him, bringing him new toys. When he was first admitted the medical staff had been really concerned that he had brain damage. In some way, for reasons they did not understand he'd had an insufficient blood supply to his brain on a temporary basis and he might not recover. That really frightened Sarah, particularly when she was told by two Doctors that they just couldn't predict the future. Fortunately Harley had fully recovered and was his normal active self in hospital and trying the nurses who had plenty of other things to attend to. Sarah would visit and stay with him most days but very much wanted to take him home so that she could carry on her normal life. Eventually she was told by the Doctors they had been unable to find any cause, but wanted to refer him for further tests that they were unable to carry out. Would she mind paying a visit to London, to Great Ormond Street Hospital, where they had all the facilities to look at unusual or difficult diseases? What they didn't tell Sarah was that Christine McBride, a social worker had phoned and spoken at length to the Consultant. She told the Consultant she was worried, there were things that did not add up about Sarah's care of the child and that she wanted to try and set up a much more extensive monitoring operation and if she could organise it, they might like to arrange covert surveillance.

The Consultant said, 'We can't do that here, but the Police may be able to help,' and Christine phoned the police.

It came as a surprise to Christine to be told that covert surveillance was a possibility and one of the ways they do this is by switching the light bulb for one with a camera built in. Their suggestion was that if the child were moved to a more specialist hospital they would liaise with whichever police force was in the area and see about installing covert surveillance. The mother would stay there with the child. On this basis Harley was to be admitted to Great Ormond Street.

The Consultant had said, 'Going to Great Ormond Street for a Munchausen Mum is like the cherry, on the icing, on the cake.'

Munchausen's Syndrome by Proxy is a former name for what is now called Fictitious or Fabricated Illness Syndrome in which parents damage the children and present it as illness; it is a particular and peculiar form of child abuse, the cause of which has not been fully established. The difficulty is that it's really not clear to what extent children may be damaged and the case of Beverley Allitt, a nurse at Grantham Hospital, who was jailed for life for killing several children is the most well-known of such cases. The Consultant was wasting his breath. Christine McBride had no idea what Munchausen's Syndrome by Proxy was. However, she liked the idea of having Harley Moss in Great Ormond Street Hospital. It offered the possibility of some excellent expense claims and paid time and transport to do some shopping in London.

Back in the office Chrissie McBride was thinking again about Sarah and Harley Moss. She was thinking about how to justify to Frances the thought that Harley's fits should be monitored. She decided she would say she had a feeling about it and was acting on that feeling. She would describe how she had persuaded the Consultant Mr Van der Merwe on the basis of social work assessment and the safety of the child as well as to support the mother. It was a gut feeling and Chrissie did a lot with gut feelings. Especially when there were good expense claims and interesting visits to be gained from them.

Great Ormond Street had no money to pay police to staff twenty-four hour surveillance. It is expensive but to save the life of a child it has to be worthwhile, so it came back to Chrissie and Frances.

As a result covert surveillance was not put into place. Harley did go with his mother to Great Ormond Street Hospital in London. They were driven there by Chrissie, whose first collection of Oxford Street bargains would be offset by a £110 wheel-clamp fine courtesy of the London Borough of Camden.

The following week Monica O'Leary was walking into Beech Lodge to see her new client, Daley Stevens. She was warmly greeted not just by the staff but by the children with whom she was very popular. Stories of her magic ability to foretell the future and to read people's palms had quickly spread among the children and they attributed to her something far beyond Local Authority Children's Services powers ever since her interaction with Daley when he was being restrained.

Daley agreed to speak to her in his bedroom. She had some reservations about interviewing a child in his bedroom. It should be a child's private place and he should be enabled to have it however he likes at such times.

Monica sat on a two-seater settee in Daley's room while Daley sat on the bed.

'Now then Daley,' she began, 'you don't seem as happy as you were. Has something happened?' She'd thought long and hard about how to approach this discussion. Subtlety wouldn't do. Straight in.

Daley looked at Monica. A minute's silence while he screwed up his face and wrinkled his nose. Then, having reached the decision he was struggling with and looking at his feet, 'Things have changed,' he said 'Alison doesn't seem to like me any more.' Monica looked. 'And?'

'And, that's it,' said Daley.

'Well, never mind that. But we will talk about it later,' Monica said. She reached into her handbag and taking out a bar of Turkish Delight, she said, 'I don't suppose you can find a home for that for me, can you? It's in there on its own and if I don't find a foster home for it, it'll sneak into my mouth while I'm not looking.' She lowered her voice, 'And I can't risk getting fat. My body's a temple, as you can probably tell.'

Daley looked up at her rotund shape, smiled and then giggled, taking the chocolate.

'Hey, hey, less of that. More respect for your social worker, please.' The tension was broken. 'Let's have a look at your art work while you dispose of that.'

Daley got out his book and began to unwrap the Turkish Delight. Monica flicked through the book and stopped on a page with a picture of an elaborate pink rose. She knew exactly what it represented.

'Daley,' slowly and intently, 'was there something you needed to tell me?' Daley looked decidedly uncomfortable.

'You can tell me.' said Monica, 'I can't guarantee I won't tell anyone but I do need to know if there's something important.'

Daley took a deep breath, his eyes alternately moving between the picture on the social worker's knee and the floor. 'I thought Alison loved me and she doesn't any more.'

'What do you mean when you say, loved, and has it got anything to do with this picture you've drawn? And what's the connection with Alison?' asked Monica.

'Just, you know, loved.'

'Well,' said Monica, 'how do you love someone?'

Daley shuffled his bottom on the bed. 'Well, you do what people who love each other do.'

'Which is?' said Monica.

'Well you…just do….personal things.'

'What personal things are we talking about? You need to understand, I do know a lot of stuff but I'm not sure what you're talking about.'

Daley took a very deep breath and was quiet for two minutes. During that time, he knew she would know anyway. She could, after all, read palms and foretell the future. When he spoke, it was almost in a whisper. 'I thought Alison loved me coz she and I did it, she let me do it to her. That's her tattoo.'

'Whoa, wait, stop,' said Monica 'Now I think I know what you're talking about and it's really not me you need to tell. You need to tell this to some special staff and have it recorded on video. It needs to be told to the Police. It's wrong and you need to tell. Would you do that for me?'

Daly thought. Two minutes silence. Three minutes silence. 'I'll do it,' he mumbled and a tear slowly meandered down his left cheek.

Half an hour later, as Monica O'Leary left Beech Lodge to return to the office to contact the Police, her right fist was clenched. 'Jaysus, Mary and Joseph, Jakey,' she whispered to herself, 'you owe me a big drink. That'll piss in their soup.'

# Seven

Police referrals are never easy to deal with. Chrissie looked at the new allocation in her basket and was disappointed. She liked best to deal with the cuddly baby referrals, those still in hospital needing adoption. It gave her the chance to cuddle a little one of the type she had always wanted, but would never have, now she had gone through the change. This referral was particularly unpleasant. A primary school teacher and scout leader who had been traced by the Police using his credit card to download pornographic images of children.

A set-back large Victorian semi with mosaic tiles on the garden path leading to a big green wooden front door. No doorbell, but instead a brass knocker. She'd waited until five o'clock to visit so as to allow him time to get in from school. She waited five minutes on the doorstep before knocking. Simon Allsop was a pleasant-looking man in his mid-to-late thirties and answered the door with a smile.

'Good afternoon,' he began, 'how can I help?'

'I'm Christine McBride. I'm a social worker from Children's Services at the Council. May I come in?'

The smile disappeared from Simon Allsop's face. Without a word, he opened the door and stood to one side, allowing Chrissie access to the house and pointing straight ahead to the kitchen.

Sitting at a pine kitchen table and facing Christine McBride, Simon began.

'I know why you've come. The Police said a social worker would turn up. Go on. Get it over with.' He looked at the social worker opposite. A very hard faced woman, certainly in her fifties or well beyond. False teeth that moved of their own volition. She made him think of a goblin.

'It's the internet thing, isn't it?'

Chrissie nodded. 'We've had a referral from the Police reporting that your name has come up on a list of men who have used a credit card to purchase obscene pictures of children from an American website, now closed down.'

'I'm a schoolteacher. I was doing some research. There are two things; I'm writing a book and also I wanted to understand what sort of things these poor little victims are subjected to. You need to understand if you have to deal with children who may have been abused...'

His voice tailed off towards the end of his explanation as he looked up to see Chrissie giving him a McBride glare.

'Speaking as one who deals with such children, I can say with authority that neither I nor my colleagues have ever recognised such a need.' Her distaste for men who downloaded child pornography showed on her face, as she went on. 'I understand you are a primary school teacher. What relevant information can you give me about voluntary or paid activity in your spare time involving children or minors?'

'I'm a Scout Assistant District Commissioner. At least I was. I resigned after the Police visited me.' Simon Allsop was very red in the face.

'Your teaching role?'

'I'm on bail. Ever since that was imposed I've been suspended. But I swear on the Holy Bible I'm not a paedophile. I'm a Christian. I have a healthy interest in working with children and...' Again he tailed off when faced with another McBride glare.

'Members of your immediate and extended family?'

'Only an elderly mother living in London. What happens now?'

'Do any children or young people visit you at all for any reason?'

'Only in my Scouting capacity.' Simon was getting angry at the apparent rudeness of this goblin-like old harpie. 'Look, I've told you that I'm not a paedophile. I would be obliged if you would let me know what happens next.'

Chrissie did not try to hide her distaste for this man. As far as she was concerned he was a pervert and public castration would only be the start of what she would like to see done with him. 'I will have to discuss with my manager whether or not we have a case conference, strategy meeting or similar and we'll get back to you. The Police will handle issues, if any, of criminality. Beyond that I can't advise you. I'll see myself out.'

As she got up to leave, Chrissie noticed a school photograph of a boy, maybe nine or ten years of age.

'Who's that?'

'Oh, for God's sake, that's my nephew. My sister's boy.' Simon was getting angrier.

'Does he visit?' Chrissie sat back down.

'On occasion.' A pause. 'You're surely not going to forbid me from seeing my family?'

'And do you have unsupervised access to him?' Chrissie was wondering how many more children visited that he had not told her about.

Suddenly Simon Allsop lost his temper. Shouting at the top of his voice, he lunged towards Christine from the other side of the kitchen. 'You Nazi cow. Get out of my house before I kill you.'

Christine's seat was near to the kitchen door. She didn't need to be told twice and left in as dignified a manner as she could manage, with her heart racing.

Having locked herself in the car, she first dialled the Police, then dialled Frances back at the office. She was overcome by nausea as she entered the office and rushed to the toilet where she was violently sick.

At exactly the same time as she was in the toilet, two uniformed Police officers were escorting Simon Allsop to the Police Station, where he would be charged with threats to kill and ultimately sentenced to a short term in prison.

In prisons, the inmates have a word for those they suspect of sex crimes. That word is Nonce and it originated with the labelling of such prisoners as non-specific offenders, shortened to nonce. They also often have strong views on how such offenders should be treated. As a result Simon Allsop never came out of prison. At the Inquest, his Death by Misadventure was attributed to him hanging himself with a bed sheet from his door handle.

Christine read about it in the local newspaper five months after her visit and was unaffected by the news.

'Could I have a word?' Monica hovered in Frances' office doorway.

Frances was not in a particularly chatty mood. She was sitting with an open file on her desk. She had been invited over to Hilary's house for dinner that evening. You've got to get it right when you're socialising with the boss and she couldn't decide whether to go smart-casual in a skirt and blouse or whether to go formal in her grey trouser suit. The last thing she needed at such an important time was Monica coming to give her some frivolous information about one of her clients.

'Just file auditing. How can I be of assistance?'

'Daley Stevens. My boy in Beech Lodge.' Monnie was starting slowly, so as to get it right.

'Ah, yes. I heard about your miraculous powers to read palms when there's a restraint. Well done.' Frances looked down at the file hoping Monnie would get the hint.

'Actually it's not to do with that, although I may have taken advantage of some prior knowledge to manipulate the situation at the time. It's much more serious.'

'Serious?' Frances hoped she wasn't going to ask for a residential transfer. She'd pulled a few strings to get Daley that placement and didn't think she'd get away with it again so soon.

'I think I've got a potential child protection situation on my hands. Daley told me he's been the subject of a sexual relationship with one of the staff. As he put it to me, he's perfectly willing to participate, even eager, but I have the impression he didn't initiate it.' Monnie stopped hovering in the doorway and sat down in the chair opposite Frances before continuing. 'It's the head of home, Alison Bryant.'

Frances suddenly felt uncomfortable. 'I don't suppose you've anything to collaborate this allegation?'

'It's corroborate you mean.'

'Whatever, but I think you'll find my command of English is accurate beyond question. What I'm asking is if you've any evidence. This is forensic social work and evidence is vital.'

Monica considered that Frances' use of the three words collaborate, accurate and forensic amounted to bullshit, but let it go, replying, 'He's willing to make a statement to the Police and do a video interview. You remember my two little twelve-year olds in Beech Lodge? Kylie and Elle? Well, they told me unprompted that Daley's shagging Alison. That's the phrase they used. Personally I think it's the other way round. There's also one other piece of evidence that can be checked.'

'Which is?'

'Which is how it started. Daley was showing me his artwork. He's very good. I asked him what a particular picture of a rose signified and he eventually told me it's a tattoo on Alison's body. I'm not absolutely sure, but I think it's quite an intimate part of her body from the way he told me. Anyway, that's ascertainable with Police and medical assistance. The point is that he's made the allegation which swings it clearly into Child Protection.'

'What I don't understand is why on earth he would tell you even if it were true given he's apparently a willing and even eager participant.' Frances looked perplexed. What teenage boy with his hormones in overdrive would complain? Jake Atkinson had written in saying something similar. He'd also named Alison Bryant. Had the department made a mistake in not investigating his claim? If that was the case, could she, Frances, be implicated in any way? It had, after all, been Hilary Campbell's decision, so she should be safe.

Her line of thought was interrupted by Monica. 'There's an easy answer there. Daley's concern is not that she's shagging him, but that she was and isn't any more. He thought she loved him and now thinks she doesn't. But whether he was a willing participant or not, it's still child sexual abuse and someone will need to investigate it. Do you want to instruct me to do that?'

'Unfortunately, I can't ask you to do it.' Frances' regret was genuine. 'Apart from the fact you'd be investigating someone senior to you, it has to be a manager who investigates child abuse allegations against staff. So I'll probably be instructed to do it myself. I do need, however, to instruct you not to say anything to anyone about this. Breach of confidentiality concerning a colleague could be a disciplinary matter. Understood?'

'Message received and understood.' Monica got up and left, barely able to conceal her delight at having successfully completed her mission which should save Jake.

Frances Phillips telephoned Hilary Campbell and relayed the information to her. Hilary was shocked and instructed Frances to personally begin an investigation immediately. She should set up and attend a video interview with the Police as quickly as possible so that they could hear what Daley had to say.

Hilary telephoned to Alison. She had thought Alison was above reproach, but had to treat as entirely separate issues the allegation about the rape and the allegation about Daley Stevens.

Alison was disappointed with the telephone call from Hilary. Hilary had explained that the allegation concerning Daley was easily proven false. All Alison needed to volunteer to do was to demonstrate that she had no tattoos.

A week later, Hilary received a letter.

*Dear Hilary,*
*Thank you for your telephone call. You will no doubt understand that after 9 years of unstinting loyalty to the Council and the children in my care, I have been devastated by the suspension. I have no criticism of you for doing it, as I fully understand the need to be seen to ensure the safety of the children in our care. It is always difficult to argue against false allegations and hard to prove you didn't do something.*
*In spite of your assurances, I can't help but feel my integrity has been called into question. Also, in a residential setting, it will be known I was suspended and it has therefore damaged my credibility with my colleagues.*

*In this situation, I feel the best thing is for me to resign. As I am under suspension, it probably will not be of any use to serve out my notice, so if the Council would wish to give me pay in lieu of notice, I will be willing to leave immediately.*

*I wish once again to stress that I am an innocent victim in this and greatly regret having to leave. Thank you for your support both over the time you have managed me and in the present situation.*

*Yours sincerely,*
*Alison Bryant.*

Hilary read the letter several times. She was half-tempted to telephone Alison and try to talk her out of leaving. To her way of thinking, Alison was an innocent victim, forced out of her job by an abusive man making false allegations and it shouldn't have been allowed to happen. There was a minor possibility Alison could have been less than professional in giving the wrong impression to the child concerned. Hilary would wait and see what came back from the Police interview. Strange things happen in social work. No point in wasting Frances' time though. In order to save needless expense, Hilary called off the investigation, with the exception of the video interview for Daley. That was, after all, the Police's expense.

Daley did speak to the Police, confirming his sexual relationship with Alison. The Police regarded it as consensual and did not take any further action. Hilary wondered if she should get Frances to call Jake in to cancel his suspension, cursing the waste of salary paid. Perhaps she would leave it for now, rather than act in haste.

Frances had sat through the interview between Daley and the Police. She had a different view from Hilary and considered that Alison was entirely culpable. When she found out Alison had been allowed to leave with pay in lieu of notice, she was furious. She needed to recognise Jake's value and determined to make his eventual return a good one.


There was a ring on the doorbell of Jake's door at home. It was midday on Wednesday. He was not expecting a visitor and was surprised to see Tom Davey standing there.

'Come on in. Tea, coffee or something stronger?'

'Thanks,' gruffly from Tom. 'Coffee, no milk, two depth chargers if you've got them.'

Fortunately for Tom, Jake kept a ready supply of sweeteners, as they were regularly favoured by some of his female friends. 'Take a seat; it's on its way.'

Tom looked around the room. A huge collection of CD's covered one wall, above which was a Bang and Olufsen Century Hi-Fi Unit. Tom approached it to look closer and as he got near, a smoked glass door slid open to reveal a console with CD player, tape player and radio.

'That's very 21st century. I'm impressed.'

'You didn't come here to talk to me about my music player, Tom. What is it?'

'Jake, you're suspended. You're a union member and you haven't rung us. Don't you want our support?' Tom sat down, by now holding a mug with a General Social Care Council logo on it.

'Here's my problem, Tom. Of course I want your support. For Christ's sake, I'm facing the prospective loss of my whole career and as far as I'm aware, I really haven't done anything wrong. I'm not going to give you my Mr Angry speech. I'm past that stage, but I don't know whether the Police are going to drop on me and charge me with rape and I am angry. Bloody angry. My boy, Daley, is being sexually abused by the Department and I'm the one suspended for bringing it up. Something stinks. It's been a fucking long time for me, even if it's only a month, give or take. And as far as I can see, it's Frances who's behind it and she's your boss as well as mine, so you could be compromising yourself if you become involved.'

'Suspension's a neutral act. It's not actually doing you any harm,' Tom considered.

'Actually that's no longer necessarily the case. I've spent the last two and a half weeks on suspension reading up my employment law. There's a case called Mezey that argues suspension isn't necessarily a neutral act. There's another older one called Gogay about a social worker unfairly suspended. I'm experiencing suspension and I can tell you it's not a free holiday. I wake up in the night sweating about losing my job. I can't take a break or a holiday in case I get a call to allow me to come back to work or call me to an investigation meeting. I don't know, like I said, if the Police will drop on me and charge me with rape. Do I need to go on?'

Tom looked Jake in the eye. 'I shouldn't tell you this, but you might wish to know that Alison Bryant hasn't agreed to give an ABE interview yet. The Police are well fed up with her and say she's got to the end of the week to make her mind up and they won't proceed without one.'

ABE or Achieving Best Evidence interviews are filmed interviews conducted in front of a video camera. They are, Jake knew from experience, always used for any potential victim who could be seen as vulnerable so that if they weren't able to give evidence at a later stage, this would be evidence on its own.

'But I have heard rumours of the possibility of another ABE interview that may have a bearing on your case. I can't tell you any more.' Tom gave a self-satisfied smile, looking at Jake as if he'd given him a real nugget of information.

'Yeah, let me give it some thought and I'll let you know if I need you to represent me.' Jake was not persuaded that Tom had either the skill or the commitment to do what was needed. And there was no way Tom would stand up to Frances. It would be like Tweetie-Pie v the Rooster out of Tom and Jerry.

'And,' Tom added, 'with two of you off like this, Frances needs to get at least one of them resolved quickly.'

And with a, 'Thanks for the coffee,' Tom left.

It was after he departed that Jake reflected on what Tom had said. Who was the other one suspended? It wasn't Tom. It couldn't be Chrissie or Sally. Monica would surely have told him if it were her. So that left Lakshmi. It could only be Lakshmi, unless of course, Monica's etiquette had caught up with her. But he'd seen Monnie only four days ago on Saturday. So it must be Lakshmi, though God only knows what for.

In the early hours of the morning Jake woke up thinking about the children and young people who had been on his caseload when he had last been at work. He was thinking about Curtis Wilson. He couldn't believe he'd been sent down for 12 months. True, he might only serve six, but he shouldn't have been sent down at all. Jake was sure Curtis had not assaulted the security man at the supermarket – the knife was still in the wrapper and the one with injuries was the boy, who had bruising all over his ribcage and stomach. Curtis's story was consistent. Jake had been suspended shortly after accompanying Curtis to court, so didn't even know whether he was coping with Young Offender's Institution. What really worried and concerned Jake was that it had been that magistrate in the Chair whose name Jake couldn't even remember – the one he'd seen on duty. Jake had gone out the day after that interview to see the daughter, Sandra Wheeler. Yes, that had been the name of the magistrate as well. Wheeler. He'd interviewed the child, Emily and her father, Darren Noble separately. He was sure that the report had been a malicious one and that the child was not at risk with Darren. She loved going to stay with him. Sandra, the child's mother hadn't been happy about his assessment and Jake wondered whether Curtis had been sent down in that way as a punishment to Jake from Wheeler, the magistrate. He hoped not.

He then started thinking about Harley Moss. There was something not right in that family. It was 3.05 am according to the projection clock's red numbers on Jake's ceiling and Jake was wide awake. He got up to make a cup of green tea. As he slowly drank it in the kitchen, he continued to think about Harley. What was it? Sarah didn't seem concerned or worn out enough by having a child with a potentially life-threatening undiagnosed condition. And she'd had her previous son die, or so she'd mentioned. Was he being stupid? She surely couldn't be somehow doing it to him? Had it been investigated? Had the previous child been investigated? He was pretty sure it wasn't Sarah, but it needed to be checked. And there was nothing he could do as he was suspended. Supposing it was indeed Sarah, the child could end up dead. Like Ricky Hegarty.

Jake still felt choked when he thought about Ricky. He would wake up in the middle of most nights thinking about Ricky. How had he fallen? What had he broken on landing? Was his death a slow painful one, or had it been mercifully quick? Jake imagined those big brown eyes glazed over in death and a broken and twisted little body.

His thoughts moved to Daley and he suddenly felt angry. Would he have reported it had he known what would happen to him? Too damned right he would have. He would fight this thing all the way and if he got dismissed from his work and had his name removed from the Social Work Register and could never work again, then so be it.

The Social Work Register. Now there was a peculiar process. Ever since 2004, social workers had been obliged to register with the General Social Care Council in order to be able to call themselves social workers and get a job. The General Social Care Council, known as the GSCC, had a reputation for being seriously inconsistent when it came to punishing social workers for misconduct. It published many of its decisions, so when someone appeared before them charged with misconduct everyone knew what they had done. There was no way of predicting what they would do with a social worker before a Conduct Committee. But it was well-known that if you went before a Conduct Committee, you would be found guilty of misconduct. It was also known that the Committees could be extremely punitive, without logical reason, unlike any other professional registration body in the United Kingdom. Doctors, nurses, veterinary surgeons, architects, chiropractors, anyone in any profession could expect consistency, but not social workers.

Social workers generally work in a blame culture, with a punitive registration body and a hostile press. You have to be committed to do the job. Maybe you should be Committed for wanting to do it.

Jake finished his green tea and began to feel as if he might sleep again. If he had difficulty, he would read some more employment law until he dozed off...

Sarah loved Great Ormond Street Hospital. She was given a side room on the ward to sleep in with Harley and was amazed by the range and number of toys available for her to use to entertain him. She sometimes spent her mornings exploring London, always spent her afternoons with Harley and she would go out most evenings after Harley had gone to sleep at seven o'clock. The tube trains of London Underground were a new experience for her. She found that if she bought a one-day Travelcard, for about £5 she could travel wherever she wanted. Sometimes, if she hadn't gone out in the morning, she'd find people standing outside the station selling the Travelcards they'd finished using for the day and could get one for £1.50 or £2.

That was how she found Camden and Camden Lock. This was an area filled with colour. People with hair of all hues, shops and stalls selling food of all types and appearances. And, as she was to later discover, the opportunity to enhance her view of everything with hallucinogenics, ecstasy and what the locals called Bob 'Ope. Weed, or draw as she also heard it called, looked a bit like a dried stock cube, but was as often as not a little harder. Sarah would learn how to use it by first heating it up with a cigarette lighter then crumbling it into tobacco which was rolled into a cigarette.

She'd met Stringbean one morning the first time she went to Camden. Stringbean was 26, a Goth and had a market stall selling Goth and smoking accessories. Stringbean, like all Goths, dressed entirely in black. He had an eyebrow pierced, as well as his lip, nose, tongue, ears and nipples.

'Now then Gorgeous, what can I do for you?' had been his first greeting to her. She was wearing her stone washed Levi's with Ugg boots and a tight white Ted Baker T-shirt.

'What's that for?' she asked, pointing to a red and gold water pipe at the back of the stall. She didn't really want to know, but did want to hear more of what this guy had to say. He was dressed all in black, with an array of piercings. Although very slim, he had well-muscled arms and as he stood up to hand the pipe across to her, she detected the exotic scent of patchouli, with a sweet, almost mysterious quality to it.

'We call it a Bong. In order to understand its magical qualities, you'll have to accompany me around the back.' He smiled and she noticed his straight white teeth and piercing blue eyes that smiled all the time. She thought she would quite like to touch the jet black hair that dropped in ringlets onto his shoulders.

'You must be kidding, a nice innocent young girl like me? You could be shipping me off to Africa as a slave, for all I know.'

'Your camel awaits. This way.' And calling to the stallholder to his right, 'Steve, watch my pitch for ten minutes or so,' he led Sarah out of the market, across the road and along an alley between two shoe shops where he unlocked a wooden door. Sarah found herself in a surprisingly spacious flat, seemingly made up entirely of stripped pine and bean bags.

'There we go. Take a seat and I'll get some coffee,' he smiled to her.

'I don't even know your name.' Sarah wondered whether to be nervous. She was a little edgy and got up as if to go.

'A thousand pardons. Welcome to my Harem. Launch pad for thousands of successful slave girls the length and breadth of North and Central Africa.' Lovely, quite posh accent and a soft easy voice. They do speak nice in London.

He took out a driving licence. 'Seriously, I'd not want you to feel insecure.' And throwing her the document he continued, 'That's me. My real name's David Kahan. It's a Polish Jewish name. Everybody calls me Stringbean, ever since my eco-protesting days when everybody had a nickname.'

Sarah quietly smiled at the thought of introducing Stringbean to her parents, or other formal settings. 'Mum, Dad, this is Stringbean...or...Do you, Stringbean, take Sarah Jennifer Moss...'

'Ok,' he said, 'so it's a little unusual. But exactly what is it that's tickled that northern sense of humour – that is a northern accent, Miss Terious? You've not given me your name either.'

Sarah blushed slightly. 'It's Sarah, Sarah Moss. And it's not North. It's Midlands, like Nottinghamshire Lincolnshire way.' Stringbean had taken out a pouch of draw, heated it and was crumbling it into some tobacco prior to putting it in the bowl of a large water pipe, a North African Shisha. He lit it, taking three deep breaths and passing the mouthpiece on a snakelike tube to Sarah.

'Pull gently. It can be a bit harsh first time.'

Sarah sucked and coughed. Not unpleasant, once you got over the coughing. Stringbean gave her a large sweet cappuccino. She had never tasted such good coffee. Ten minutes later, as she walked back across to the market, the colours smells and sounds seemed just slightly more vibrant than when she had left. She also was beginning to feel really hungry.

'Come back and see me again,' Stringbean smiled as she headed for Chalk Farm station.

'I might just do that.' And she returned to Great Ormond Street Hospital, where it was time to give Harley his lunch.

Naren didn't have any flowers with him this Thursday, but did bring a bottle of German Spatlëse wine, which he uncorked and put in the fridge. Having inspected the contents of the fridge, he closed the door.

'How's my lovely Lakhi?' he asked patting her bottom and winking. Lakshmi looked down in her customary way and smiled.

'Come upstairs with me, we have important things to consider and I have some excellent news.'

'Why does excellent news have to be given upstairs?' Lakshmi had a shrewd idea that she knew exactly why. She complied anyway. A good Hindu wife-to-be shouldn't really act like a good Hindu wife before they are married, but she would think about that another time.

Naren lacked subtlety in the intimacy of the bedroom. Today was no different. Once upstairs, he pulled at her clothes with such haste she was afraid he would tear them. Her salwar kameez was more tailored than some she had. They never came off easily, in spite of the elasticated waist on the salwar part of the suit.

'Not so quickly.' Tilting her head to one side and lifting the kameez, 'Wouldn't you rather I undressed slowly?' giving a seductive smile.

His eyes narrowed. 'Fucking bitch, when I give instruction it's to be done,' and he pushed her roughly on the bed.

Looking at her body, he motioned towards her crotch and continued, 'And that's not good enough. You need a Bollywood. Go see Zainab. Muslim girl in salon on high street. She'll sort it. I want picture.' He had his Pentax Optio in his hand before she could object. 'Move hands. You have to be less inhibited. Maybe we must let Nikhil watch. It'll be good for him.'

Lakshmi said nothing. Naren sometimes got angry easily while engaged in sexual acts. Sometimes he liked to talk in the most graphic terms about what he was doing and wanted her to do the same. At such times it seemed to be a turn-on for him. Lakshmi couldn't bring herself to join in and she chose to put up with his taunts of being prudish. At other times he was kind, attentive and gentle whispering to her in Hindi, their language of love. This was one of his less gentle days.

A half hour later, he briefly left the bedroom coming back with two glasses of Spatlëse by now cold. It was crisp and fruity. You could almost taste the grapes and it had a slightly nutty, almost almondy tang, Lakshmi thought. It was delicious.

They toasted the future and Naren began with, 'It's time you had changed the will to make me executor. I can't ensure Nikhil's protection in the future if it ever becomes necessary if you don't change it. It'll probably never be necessary, but we never know what's around the corner. I'm thinking of you and Nikhil.'

Lakshmi had a slight stomach ache. Monica from the office would have known how to sort it. She cured everybody's ills and even foretold their future. She smiled, remembering a story about Monica and a restraint in a children's home that she'd stopped by reading the child's palm. A sudden nausea came over her and she rushed to the bathroom and threw up. She really needed to have a pregnancy test and would probably have to consider a termination if it was positive.

She was still daydreaming ten minutes later, back on the bed, wrapped in her purple hooded dressing gown, when Naren, beaming announced, 'And now the good news. I've arranged a way of getting rid of the audit investigation, so you won't have to bother about it. It's all sorted.'

Lakshmi was delighted. 'How have you managed that?'

Naren hesitated, very slightly. 'All you have to do is give me a payment, which I know you can afford, I pass it on to them and they find there is no case to answer.' He beamed at the simplicity of his plan.

'How much?' Lakshmi's heart sank. This was corruption and she could not be comfortable being part of it.

'Twenty-Five.' Pause. 'Thousand, of course. They wanted much more but I told them you couldn't afford any more. It'll still leave you with about ten thousand.' It seemed so simple to him. Lakshmi was amazed on several levels. How could he think she was so corrupt as to consider buying her way out of the situation? Did he honestly think she would give a penny of her hard-earned savings to some sleazy bent official, when it would be taking food out of her son's mouth? And how the hell did he know how much savings she had? He had been absolutely accurate. Then she was furious.

'I think you should leave my house. Now. I won't give them a penny. Let them accuse me of whatever they want. Let them send me to prison. Get out and don't come back. The relationship is over. I don't want to see you again.' Lakshmi's anger was plain. Surprised, Naren got dressed as quickly as he could and left rapidly.

Lakshmi went to her shrine room and as she quietly meditated, she thought she saw the letter 'J' reflected by the light on the shrine. She meditated more and when she finished she was sure she must speak to someone whose name was Jay or started with J.

As she got up, she felt sick again and remembered she needed to go to the chemist. She went to the toilet again before heading to the chemist, where she bought a home pregnancy kit. At home, she weed into a small bottle and dipped the wand. To her relief the test was negative. She returned to the toilet.

# Eight

Jake had heard nothing of what was happening with his suspension. He was angry and he ran daily. Hard. It was a Tuesday in late August and he was finishing a run at eleven in the morning when a car pulled up next to him, a Volkswagen Polo in silver. He looked in and there was sitting Lakshmi Patel.

'Jake?' He looked across and stopped, surprised to see Lakshmi. 'Jake, I need to speak to you.'

Jake was sweaty as he got into the car. 'Drive me round the corner to my place and we'll chat.'

Once inside he sat Lakshmi down. 'Something to drink?'

'I don't suppose,' she said, 'you would have such a thing as green tea?'

'It just so happens,' said Jake, 'that I do. I'll make you some.'

Jake had a quick shower, got changed and made them both a large cup of green tea. Just a pinch of leaves in each cup, fill with boiling water and wait until the leaves sink.

'What are you doing here Lakshmi?' he inquired.

She answered, 'I've been suspended and I know it's you I have to speak to.'

'So have I,' said Jake, 'but I'm not supposed to speak to anyone.'

'I'm not supposed to speak to anyone either but my God tells me I have to speak to someone who's name begins with J.'

It had taken her some time to think of everybody she knew whose name began with J and Jake's name came into her head again and again and again.

'Jake I don't know why I'm speaking to you and there are things I can't tell you because I can't tell them to a man, particularly a white man.' She thought for a minute. 'No, that came out wrong.' I meant to a non-Hindu, no... I don't know what I meant, but it's too embarrassing.'

Jake said, 'I'm happy to help if I can and I have a friend, whom you know, who I'm sure would help us and would listen to what you have to say. A woman.'

'That would be so helpful,' said Lakshmi. 'As I said, it's embarrassing... it's difficult and I don't really know where to go with it.'

And she started to tell Jake her story. Her story about meeting Naren. She admitted, uncomfortably that she'd met him over the internet. She said he'd treated her badly, but wouldn't give him information. She told him about the audit investigation and the amount of information that Naren seemed to know. She told him that he had taken money and said he had wined and dined the Audit Department. She said, 'And now he's going to disgrace me and get me cut off from my family, what with information and dishonesty and pictures and all.'

It was the word, 'pictures,' that Jake noticed, although he didn't ask.

'Why,' he said casually, 'don't I get hold of this other person, see if she'll spare us some time? She will be familiar and we can meet on Saturday.'

'I'll look forward to that,' said Lakshmi. 'Thank you Jake.'

Jake phoned Monnie, who listened to a very brief version on the telephone. She said nothing, until Jake asked, 'Are you still there?'

'Feckin cont,' she answered, 'I'd fry his bollocks myself. And talking about fried bollocks, why don't the pair of you come for a meal on Saturday? I'm on my own because Pat's away in Birmingham, so I'd welcome the company.'

Jake relayed the question to Lakshmi, who said, quietly, 'Is it okay even if I'm a vegetarian?'

He turned back to the phone. 'It'll have to be a different menu as she's a non-meat eater.'

'Vegetarian fried bollocks it is.' Monica was obviously on form today. 'One o'clock?' Jake got Lakshmi's agreement and confirmed it.

The concept of a friend of the opposite gender was a strange one for Lakshmi. For her, as a devout Hindu woman, the only man outside the family with whom you have a relationship is your husband or husband-to-be. Ideally that would be like a brother/sister relationship to make it entirely pure. You don't associate with other men. It's the way it's always been and the way it will always be.

Monica's modern bungalow was decidedly cottagey. The old English rose growing up the porch was in full glorious bloom and an apple tree was a few weeks yet away from picking. Monica's lawn had wavy edges and there were pots of marigolds and petunias dotted around the outside of the house. Inside, cut glass chandelier drops hung in the windows, projecting rainbows all over the front room as the sun hit them. Photographs of two handsome young men and a petite beautifully even-featured young woman in her late teens or early twenties adorned several shelves. Another photograph, which Jake wrongly thought showed the same beautiful young woman arm in arm with the darker-haired of the young men was on the wall.

'Your kids?' Jake asked.

Monnie pointed to the couple. 'That's me and Pat when we married. The others are the kids.'

Jake and Lakshmi were amazed by the similarity between parents and children and as he looked at Monica, he could see the same smiling eyes in the photograph that he knew so well. Jake and Lakshmi sat in the deep chintz chairs and Lakshmi told Monica the same story she had told to Jake on Tuesday. Jake announced an intention to inspect the garden with a cigar, so Lakshmi could open up. When he returned a half hour later, Monica was sitting on the sofa with her arm round Lakshmi. They had both been crying.

Monica said as Jake came in, 'Now I've heard it all. Lakhi (she pronounced it 'Lucky') has said I can repeat it all to you. We'll sort it together.'

Jake had spent the time between Tuesday and Saturday looking up Employment Law and he'd at long last bought his own copy of Selwyn's Law of Employment from the local bookshop. He was ready.

Without warning, Monica jumped up and ran out. 'Shit, shit, shit, shit, shit, shit.'

'What is it?' Jake and Lakshmi followed her out the room.

'The feckin' dinner will be cremated.' Jake and Lakshmi found her in the kitchen, bent over the oven. She pulled out a Denby oval roaster full of something sizzly. 'Saved by the smell. Vegetable lasagne. Don't know about you, but I could eat a black snake with a festered arse. Tuck in. It'll sort your jiffly tum,' winking at Lakshmi.

'Jacob, listen now. I've got a serious question. We're off to France.' Monnie was looking intently at Jake. They were relaxed in the lounge, full of lasagne followed by profiteroles and washed down with a young Bordeaux, the three of them comfortably sleepy. 'How do you say, 'can I use my credit card to buy all these crates of booze?'? I'll bet you speak French because you're so Bay Window.'

Jacob thought for a minute.

Lakshmi looked up. 'In Gujerati it's, 'Aahr card vapri shaku chu?' and in Hindi it's, 'Mei ye card vapar shakti hui?''

'And in French if you show them your credit card and say, 'Ça suffit?' you'll get by,' added Jake.

'Why would I need bloody Gujerati and Hindi? I'm not going that far east.' Monica sat up.

Lakshmi was quick on the uptake, 'It could be an Indian shop. Bordeaux, Gauloises and Poppadoms.'

After the laughter from all three died down, Monica said, 'Seriously now, Jake what was it again?' She had it off to a tee after twenty minutes and promised to report back to Jake whether it worked.

As Jake shared the story of the events leading up to his suspension, Lakshmi was wide-eyed.

Jake wasn't sure whether to be totally open about his relationship with Alison, so he asked. 'I'm not sure about telling you all the details, as it's embarrassing and very personal and,' looking at Lakshmi, 'some people in the room are very refined and may not be used to the type of details I need to give.'

Monica was aware of the information Jake needed to give and came in with, 'Don't you worry your pretty head, thick bastard, she'll effingwell tell anyone to fuck off if she needs to. I've heard her. She just thinks you're too innocent to hear it. Isn't that right darling?'

Lakshmi looked slightly embarrassed and nodded. 'We Hindu women watch what we say in front of men. It's an unspoken rule to give the impression of purity. But when did you last meet a social worker in Child protection who hadn't heard all the language and been called most of it? It's just when you're Asian they refine it. Like they say in those posh food adverts, This is not just an ordinary interfering old cunt. This is an interfering old Paki cunt. And I've never even been to Pakistan. So you fire away.' She laughed, feeling as if she had been liberated.

So Jake told it, in all its gory detail, with the drink in the pub, the lovemaking, the tattoo, the whispers from FCUK and pink-knickers at Beech Lodge, Daley's artwork and the whistleblowing letter prior to his suspension.

Lakshmi flinched. 'It must be so painful. I couldn't have a tattoo there, even if I was willing for anyone to see me undressed like that.' And she crossed her legs tightly and shuddered.

She paused and thought for a minute. 'Can I share some personal detail? It's embarrassing.' They both nodded.

Looking down, she said, 'Naren told me to go and have a Bollywood done. I had no idea what he meant, so I went to the shop he told me to go to. You wouldn't believe what it is?' She was right. Neither Monnie nor Jake had ever heard of it. 'Have you ever heard of a Brazilian Wax?'

Jake said nothing although he had.

Monica said, 'It's no use speaking to me about such things. Even in the days before I stopped wearing a belt I couldn't see my nether regions for many years and if you can't admire your purchases what's the point?'

Lakshmi continued, 'Well, a Bollywood's a Brazilian with Henna tattoo pattern added.'

'Did you have it done?'

'Monica!' Jake's tone was one of exaggerated rebuke. 'Don't you think that's a bit personal?'

Before Monnie could answer, Lakshmi laughed, saying, 'Get it done? Not on your bloody nelly. Nor on mine. But worst of all he wanted to take pictures.'

'And did he?' Lakshmi drifted thoughtfully into silence.

'And did you say he'd got six properties?'

'Uh-huh', dipping her finger in the profiterole sauce on the serving plate they hadn't managed to empty.

'And he's been trying to persuade you to change your will?' Jake was suddenly very alert. 'If he got those properties the same way, where are the previous owners?'

Monica and Lakshmi realised what he was asking.

Lakshmi stopped, a finger full of Sauce Suchard mid-air. 'What can I do about it?'

'Check the internet and see what you can find on him. You never know.'

And none of them in their wildest dreams could have imagined what she would discover.

Curtis Wilson spent six weeks in a Young Offender's Institution. His case was reviewed after Charles Osbourne, the fifteen-year-old son of a black Member of Parliament complained he and two friends had been assaulted by supermarket security staff at Megasave just a week after Curtis went to Wetherby. It was strongly denied by Megasave, but they had been unaware of the other young man with them, who filmed it on his mobile phone. As a result, several cases were reviewed, Curtis among them.

He was surprised on arriving home to find a large pan of oxtail and butterbean stew, rice 'n' peas and callaloo cooking on a sparkling clean stove.

'What happen here mam?'

Dolly smiled. She was dressed in a floral dress with a lace collar, starched and ironed. 'Well, son, it's like this. You got sent to children's prison and they sent the social worker and two doctors to see me. Two doctors. Can you believe it? I got sectioned into hospital for twenty-eight days. They tell me I got schizophrenia and gave me medication. All I do is take pills, pills, pills.' She paused, sighed and said, 'Mmmm, Mmmm. My, My.' and paused again. 'My voices weren't real, y'know. They're gone. All I got to do is take the pills every day. Then when I came home I saw what a mess the house was in, how dirty the cooker is. So I spent the last two weeks doing nothing but clean. But I been cooking as well, just like I always used to...'

She faded as she saw Curtis was in tears and put her arms around him for the first time in twelve years.

It was an overcast morning. Lakshmi was at home, making parathas. She was thinking of the story from Hindu mythology of Draupadi, Arjun and Duhsasana. She had been thinking of how Monica, a married woman had the freedom in her culture to come and go as she chose, to be friends with Jake and to speak as openly as she did. Monnie, a Roman Catholic, also had religion, but it seemed a much more relaxed way of life than Lakshmi's Hindu upbringing allowed.

The story of Draupadi is written in the Mahabharata, the epic Hindu poem. Her story has many aspects to it and Lakshmi was thinking about Draupadi and her place in society as a Hindu woman. The Mahabharata tells that

Draupadi was a wonderfully beautiful woman, lovely enough to have come from the city of the gods. Her hand was sought by many princes and so her father determined to hold a competition or (as they call it) a swayamvara and allow her to exercise her own choice in the selection of a husband. The swayamvara was announced and princes came from all over to compete. Although the final choice would rest with Draupadi, it was expected that she would choose the winning contestant as her husband. Prince Arjuna competed along with his four brothers. With his unbelievable skill as an archer, he became the selected bridegroom.

When the five brothers returned to their mother Kunti they told her that they had made a great acquisition in winning the hand of Draupadi. She told them they must share their good fortune. These words presented a difficult problem, for if they could not be discreetly sidestepped they would have to be obeyed. They consulted Vyasa, a renowned sage. He settled the matter declaring that the destiny of Draupadi had already been decided by the gods and she was destined to become the wife of all the brethren. So she became their common wife and it was arranged that she should stay successively in the house of each and that not one of them but the master of the house should enter it while she was there. No mention (as far as Lakshmi was aware) of what Draupadi thought of this deal, but Lakshmi knew that Arjuna was Draupadi's favourite of the brothers and that the arrangement was made. As Monica would have said, variety is the spice of married life.

At an organised gambling match in Hastinapura the Elephant City, Yudhisthira played against his cousins, the Kauravas. He lost everything, so he, his kingdom, his brothers and their wife Draupadi were indebted to the Kauravas. They included Duryodhana and Duhsasana. So in this way, Draupadi became enslaved to the Kauravas. One day Duryodhana called her to come and sweep the room. She refused. Duhsasana dragged her by the hair into the pavilion before all the chieftains and tauntingly told her that she was a now slave girl and had no right to refuse or complain of anything, including being touched by men. He said that a whore who has five husbands has no honour and might as well be naked in public. As he pulled at and tore her sari in front of everyone she prayed to Lord Krishna. Krishna protected her and magically, her garments were replaced as fast as they were torn. The depictions tend to show Duhsasana unwinding her sari at one end while Krishna magically adds to the material at the other. Eventually, Duhsasana gave up and Draupadi's dignity was retained.

Lost in parathas, Draupadi and Monica's way of life, Lakshmi was slightly startled when the telephone rang. She was surprised to hear Naren's voice. Lakshmi's five month relationship was over, as far as she was concerned. Lakshmi reminded Naren of this and also the fact that whatever he had said about his divorce, it hadn't happened and she didn't believe it was about to. She told him she was not going to be anyone's possession, mistress, bit on the side, or (and she thought of Draupadi) slave and said his priority should be his daughters, one of whom was due to get married.

Naren was apologetic over the telephone. He protested that he really was going to get a divorce and he had the court papers to prove that all he was waiting for was the Decree Absolute.

'Please let me come over and show the papers to you. I also have something you have to see. It will help your case with the Council more than you could ever imagine. I love you and I can't live without you.' Something in his tone sounded very sincere.

Lakshmi's tone was cold and she told him he was not coming to her home, not now or again, but she was curious. She arranged to meet him at Megasave, about half a mile from her home. Her intention was to sit and have a cup of coffee and let him show her whatever papers he had.

She drew into the supermarket car park where Naren was standing outside. She climbed out of her car and he motioned over to a black car which he asked her to get into. She refused, saying they should go into the café as she had planned.

'I just wanted to talk. The café is so public and if you would sit in the car I will show you what I wanted you to see. It's very important and the privacy will also allow me to tell you my true feelings,' he responded.

Lakshmi's curiosity got the better of her. She climbed into the front passenger seat of the car. Her sari was a little long and she had to be careful to gather it up. Naren like a true gentleman, held open the passenger door and having gently pushed it closed, he walked round and climbed into the driver's seat. It was a Toyota Avensis, with a rich smell of leather and big comfortable seats. After climbing in, Naren immediately started the engine and drove out of the supermarket car park.

Surprised, Lakshmi asked, 'Where are you going?'

'I have pain in my stomach. I could do with a toilet,' he answered.

'What's wrong with the toilet in Megasave? It's clean and over there.' Lakshmi was not comfortable with going elsewhere, especially as she had not locked her car. Naren said nothing, but continued to drive. As they passed McDonald's, between Megasave and Lakshmi's house he once again said he wanted to use the toilet.

'McDonald's is just there. They're always busy, so no-one will notice if you go in just for the loo.' He ignored it and drove to Lakshmi's house. She was mildly annoyed.

'I told you over the phone I wasn't going to have you over and I meant it.' Lakshmi felt she was being set up, but she was not sure for what.

Naren got out of the car and was walking up and down in front of Lakshmi's house, shouting, 'I'm in pain. I need to go inside.' And louder, 'I'm in unbearable pain.'

Thinking he would disturb the neighbours, Lakshmi found it rather embarrassing. She was right. Neighbours on both sides and across the road had moved their net curtains to look. She opened the front door.

'After you've been, take me back to my car. And don't leave the seat up.' She followed him in and to her surprise he didn't go upstairs to the toilet, but walked straight into the kitchen.

She followed him into the kitchen. 'Where are you going? The toilet's upstairs.'

Without a word, he opened his briefcase and took out a document. It wasn't a court paper, but was Lakshmi's Curriculum Vitae, which she had given only to the Council when she originally applied for a job there. Highlighted in yellow was the phrase where she had written that she had lived with a Muslim. She hadn't intended it to mean that she had had an intimate relationship with a Muslim, but it was true that Yasser Ibrahim had been one of her lodgers for a while. She considered that as a Hindu woman it demonstrated an awareness of cultural diversity and a tolerance of different religious or ethnic groups. Hindus and Muslims are generally considered not to be compatible. Naren had clearly not understood her intention in writing it.

His voice was loud and angry when he spoke. 'You bitch. You lied. You were living with Moslem.'

He started slapping her around the face with an open hand. Lunging forward, he pushed Lakshmi, forcing her to sit on a high wooden kitchen chair, as he continued shouting, 'No Hindu man would ever accept you have been used by a Moslem.'

He appeared even more agitated and angry as he continued. He swore in Gujerati, using the filthiest words she knew. 'Bhoslini. Bhenchod. Madarchod.' His voice became louder as he spat out each word.

In spite of her increasing sense of fear and shock at being called the worst type of fucking cunt, she briefly wondered how he could label her, a woman, as a sister fucker and a mother fucker. Her shock was increased and her fear heightened as Naren continued to slap her around the face and, missing as she successfully moved her head to duck a blow, he kicked her in the leg leaving a muddy mark on her favourite lilac and white sari. The pallu, that part of the sari draping her shoulder slipped down and Naren reached forward to grab her lilac blouse, tearing it open at the front to expose her bra.

He shouted, 'You didn't tell me. Was it Yasser or was it another? How many Moslems did you have?'

How did he know Yasser's name? She had only told it to the audit investigators. Briefly and embarrassed at her semi-naked state, Lakshmi's thought went back to the story of Draupadi. She prayed silently and urgently to Krishna.

Naren was flushed, with beads of sweat on his forehead and his moustache glistening. He looked down at Lakshmi's now exposed bra.

This seemingly angered him further, as he shouted, 'How many times have I told you not to wear a bra when you see me?' Yelling, 'Take them off', he pulled at both the torn blouse and bra.

Lakshmi realised Krishna was not going to intervene and reached behind her to undo the bra clip to prevent more damage and pain. The clothing was thrown onto the kitchen floor. By now Lakshmi was very frightened and thought Naren might kill her. .

She was feeling the cold. She had goose bumps on her arms and bare breasts. She got off the chair.

Naren said, in a venomously threatening tone, 'Where are you going? You'll stay where I tell you to.' He pulled the chair to face him and pushed her back onto the chair. As he did so he put his hands between her knees to force them apart, making her sari ride up and revealing a pair of lilac high-waisted briefs. Pulling on them by the waistband, he said quietly, 'Take them off.' Lakshmi slipped on the chair and nearly fell off it. As this happened, he pulled down her pants, which stopped at her jewelled shoes, 'Take them off too.' Menacingly. She stood on the floor to bend down and undo them. As she bent down, Naren pushed her head further down with one hand and undid his trouser zip with the other. He then pulled her head backwards by the hair and pushed his penis into her mouth. Although it was initially flaccid, it went hard. He yelled, 'Take it all in your fucking mouth.' She retched and he jerked her hair backwards, pulling out a handful as she gasped with pain. He didn't leave it in her mouth for long and didn't ejaculate. Pulling it out of her mouth, he pushed her back onto the chair and forced her legs apart again. By this time Lakshmi's fear had increased immeasurably. Having forced apart her legs, his nails digging into her thighs, he pushed his midriff towards her to push his penis inside her dry vagina, but could not get it in. Bruised and in more pain, Lakshmi pleaded with him not to do it, saying that as there were no curtains the neighbours could see in and might be watching. Naren then pulled her off the chair, unwound her sari and threw it on the floor. Lakshmi was left standing only in her underskirt. He pushed her through into the next room and onto the floor by her Hindu shrine.

'Fucking bitch. I'll give you a lesson.' Lakshmi lay on the floor with her head just touching the base of the patio door. He had one leg out of his cream coloured trousers and his blue loose-fitting boxer shorts.

He went on, still shouting, 'So you like Moslems. Pretend I am Yasser.' Lakshmi was sure at this stage he was going to kill her. Pinning her down by holding both wrists with his left hand and putting his undressed leg across hers, he removed his trousers and pulled his shirt up with his right hand. His legs and stomach were hairy and he smelled of stale sweat and garlic-flavoured halitosis. He then forced her legs apart using his legs to do so and lay on top of her.

'Stop. This is rape. You are raping me. It is not right.' He hit her face again on the left cheekbone, this time with a closed fist. With difficulty, Lakshmi stayed silent.

He forced his penis into her still dry vagina, with evident difficulty. Already bruised there, she felt it tear as he reached down to use his right hand to force apart her labia. He leered as Lakshmi winced and tried to kick until she didn't feel able to struggle any more She then turned her head to look at a statue of Lord Shiva and prayed silently. It was not long before she smelled semen, felt greasy inside and knew he had ejaculated. After this, he appeared to calm down and rolled off her. She waited for a minute or two trying to work out whether she was safe. Naren was lying quietly next to her in a trance-like state.

'Please,' she whispered, 'I need to pee.' The laminate floor had traces of blood, semen and sweat on it and the patio door base had blood and snot from Lakshmi's left nostril. He nodded, almost imperceptibly.

Hoping she would be safe to do so, Lakshmi gingerly got up. She hurt all over, her head throbbed and she felt sick. She went upstairs into the toilet, where she locked the door, cried, vomited and washed her face. She then spent about twenty minutes in the shower with the water as hot as she could bear, the shower head held to her crotch trying to wash away the dirty feeling. Her crotch was tender, bruised and bleeding from where it had been torn in the assault. She dressed in joggers and a tee-shirt and returned downstairs feeling numb. To her relief, Naren had left.

Lakshmi went through to the kitchen and picked up her favourite lilac and white sari, lilac blouse, underwear and jewelled shoes, walked into the back garden and dropped them in the bin.

# Nine

It was seven-thirty and Wednesday. Good news for Jake. Only a half hour of Grumpies on TV instead of the regular two hours or more. The doorbell rang. Three times.

'Monica O'Leary, what are you doing at this time of night in this neck of the woods?'

'Jake, I need a word with you. Now I want you to listen. Don't say a feckin' word. Don't fart. Just listen.'

And she started to tell him about Daley's picture and her chat with him. As she finished relating her visit to Beech Lodge the week before, Jake was lost for words. He welled up.

'Monica, I owe you. So what happens next?'

'Too bloody right you owe me. I was looking forward to that Turkish Delight bar and I wasted it on the boy because of you.'

'What Turkish Delight bar?' Jake was puzzled.

'Oh, did I leave that bit out? I bribed him with a Turkish Delight bar. Up until then his lips were sealed tighter than a novice nun in a chastity belt.'

'And now?'

'Daley does his video tomorrow. And I've had to tell the Ayatollah. How the feck was I supposed to do that? Frances, I was just discussing Ms Bryant's minge with my new client and you'll never guess what sort of tattoo he told me she's got?'

Jake's more serious reply was, 'How about I think I've got a serious and very sensitive child protection issue I've got to bring to your attention. And for goodness sake I hope you didn't mention you know anything about me or my situation.' He paused. 'You can get suspended for daring to mention the possibility of such things.'

'That's pretty much what I did and I'm still there. Although, coming to think of it I wouldn't mind being paid to sit around on my arse all day like you and that other lucky bastard, Lakshmi.' She stopped for a while. Both were thinking about Daley Stevens.

Jake noticed Monica had tears in her eyes. She sniffed and took a well-used paper tissue out of her bag. 'He's a lovely lad. Thick as a whale omelette, but so good-natured. He didn't deserve this, especially when we take them in with the aim of protecting them. It's not his fault he's a young Adonis and he doesn't even realise how fecking wrong it is. The cow. The filthy bitch.' Her sorrow was turning to anger and Jake could feel another tirade approaching, when the doorbell rang again.

Jake was surprised to see Lakshmi, out of breath and looking afraid. He ushered her in and she stopped, as she saw Monnie in the lounge.

'I'm sorry, I didn't know you had company,' she began, when Monica interrupted.

'I turned up on spec also and we've been talking about you, but if you want him to yourself…' and she winked.

'No, I'm really pleased you're here as well. I wanted to show you what I turned up from my internet research.' She handed Jake a piece of A4 paper and Jake looked briefly.

'Oh. My. God.' As Jake read it, the colour drained from his face.

'What?' asked Monica.

Jake, still very pale, began to read out loud, 'In the Nottingham Crown Court before His Honour Mr Justice Rowbotham QC. Regina v Naren Bhargava. 8th May 2003. That's some years ago now. It's a transcript of a Court Hearing,' and flicking through, 'he got eight years for seven counts of assault, including two of rape and administering a noxious substance, namely arsenic, with intent to endanger life. It was a woman this refers to as his mistress who was the victim, although he was married.'

Turning to Lakshmi, he said, 'And it's him?'

'Without question. Same date of birth. Same name. Same address.' They sat in silence for a full five minutes.

'Well,' said Monica, almost whispering, 'that'll explain your shits and pukes. I didn't think your jiffly tum was normal. But I thought it was something to do with you being a bloody vegetarian. That'll teach me to be culturally sensitive.' Bursting into tears, she almost ran across the room and threw her arms around Lakshmi, who was also in tears. Jake sat and read again the transcript.

The following Saturday, two women were walking from shop to shop. One short stout Irish woman and the other, an Indian woman, taller and slim. 'It's a business suit she wants,' was the shorter woman's greeting to each shop assistant, 'as slick as you can do for a tenner.'

Seventeen shops later, Lakshmi had purchased three suits, four blouses and two pairs of shoes with branded French underwear to match. Monica's ten pound budget had long since been abandoned, if she had ever been serious about it in the first place.

As they sat both drinking Cappuccino in a café, surrounded by assorted carrier bags, Monica leaned across, 'We're ready to shove bangers up their arses.'

Back at home, two days later on Monday morning, Lakshmi was re-examining her purchases. As she tried her second suit on and turned in front of a mirror, the telephone rang. It was the Head teacher from Nikhil's Hindu school, Mr Kothari.

'Miss Patel, I'm in a very difficult position. Could you possibly spare the time to come in and see me?'

Fifteen minutes later and still in her new pinstriped suit, Lakshmi walked through the school doors and across the polished floor. Her new shoes were slippery on the floor and she had to walk carefully. She was also walking uncomfortably because of her clutching stomach pains. She did not know whether they were as the result of stress or if, as she was beginning to suspect, they were something much more sinister.

'Come in, come in. Please take a seat.' Lakshmi sat, thinking this must be a regular event for miscreants in the school and hoped desperately that Nikhil was not one of them. From out of his desk, Mr Kothari took a letter which he handed to Lakshmi without comment. She read,
*Dear Sir,*
*As a conserned bystander, I am writting to you about Miss LAKSHMI PATEL who's behavior is a danger to her lovely young son NIKHIL. Most nights she has wild parties with her sister PUJA, where drugs are taken openly and there is sex with loads of men. This is not the sort of background you want boys in your school from.*
*Singed,*
*A Conserned Bystander*

'Miss Patel, I'm not concerned about the information in the letter, as I know you better than that. I'm not impressed with the spelling. However...' and he took a deep breath before continuing, 'we have been also receiving daily anonymous telephone calls about you, no doubt from the same man. And it is a man. He can be quite abusive, goes on for quite a long time and disturbs the junior staff. We don't want to lose Nikhil, but I need to think of the overall welfare of everyone in the school. Can you cast any light on the situation?'

Lakshmi was quiet for several minutes. When she spoke, it was quietly and with an anger and strength the teacher had never seen before. 'His name is Naren Bhargava. He is an unpleasant and a dangerous man who has been stalking and harassing me for a while. Please be patient. I will sort it out shortly either via the Police or via injunction or maybe even both.'

'We will do all we can at this school to help you over the next few weeks. But we will need a resolution in that time.'

'Trust me,' said Lakshmi, a pinpoint of anger in her dark eyes, 'it won't take that long.'

And she returned to her car.

If there was one thing Sally hated it was a referral concerning an alcoholic. Yet here she was on a wet Monday afternoon, standing outside a pine-cladded semi-detached 1960s monstrosity of a house with the paint peeling off the cladding. As the door opened, there was the unmistakeable smell of vomit. A pathetic wreck of a woman stood in front of her, sporting a Lady Clairol and Evostick coiffure. No make-up and thin. A figure like a twiglet. Thirty-five to forty, maybe?

'Elaine Wrattray?' Wrattarsed, more-like. A nod and pursed lips. 'I'm Sally Beckett. I'm a social worker from Children's Services at the Council. May I come in?' Not a word. The door opened and Sally followed Elaine into the lounge.

She stood. 'Perhaps we could have the television turned off.' Done. 'We have some concerns about Emily, your six-year old. We have had a report that she is insufficiently fed and clothed and wondered if you would consent to her being seen by a paedriatrician.'

Elaine Wrattray raised her right hand to point at Sally. 'Don't you go accusing me of not looking after my daughter. You're barely old enough to have children, so you've no business to go around telling others how they should do it.' Her voice was quietly threatening and below the unkempt appearance was a surprisingly well-educated accent. 'I will be happy to consent. I will take her myself. I will not tolerate unannounced visits wherein neglect by me is implied. Please leave and come back with some authority. Alternatively make an appointment. You no doubt have my telephone number on file. Good day.'

Sally left.

On her return to the office, she approached Frances. 'Elaine Wrattray. What's her background?'

'Legally qualified. Solicitor or barrister. Can't remember which. Went to pieces after her divorce. Nasty piece of work.'

Sally returned to her desk to write a letter.

*Dear Ms Wrattray,*

*Following my visit to you today, I have to emphasise the concerns which have been brought to our attention by Emily's Head Teacher. If you would therefore kindly attend our offices at 2.30 next Thursday I will be pleased to discuss with you prospective ways forward so as to avoid the need for formal action on our part.*

*Yours sincerely,*

*Sally Beckett,*

*Social Worker*

At 2.30 on the following Thursday, Sally was at her desk, completing file notes.

'I'll lay two quid she doesn't turn up.' Sally looked up to see Tom, who continued, 'And what are you going to do then?'

'I'm bloody hoping she does. The last thing I want to do is Child Protection on Emily. She's a pathetic little thing and any interview will probably terrify her. But I can't leave that human stick insect not feeding her or collecting her from school while she's on the piss. And what sort of pattern does it set for her in the future? Anyway…' The conversation was interrupted by Sally's telephone.

'Mrs Wrattray's in reception to see you.' There was something in Sue's tone that hinted at surprise.

On her arrival in reception, Sally was surprised to see Elaine Wrattray, dressed in a navy well-cut suit, heels and full, if subtle make-up.

'Good afternoon, Mrs Wrattray and thank you for coming. I assume you received my letter. Please come into the interview room.' She followed Elaine Wrattray into the small office and began, 'As you are aware we have had some contact from Emily's school.'

'May I interrupt you?' A soft and polite interjection from the suited Elaine. Sally noticed that her nails had been professionally manicured, her 15 denier tights were subtly coloured to match her suit and her Jane Shilton handbag was pristine.

'I realised after your last visit and your letter that I have to take stock of my situation. I know I was somewhat short with you, for which I apologise. I have decided to acknowledge that I am an alcoholic and must change. I can't risk losing Emily. In the nine days since I've seen you; I've joined Alcoholics Anonymous. I've now been sober for four days. What I came here to ask is that I get a second chance and that you don't take Emily away.'

'Mrs Wrattray…'

'Please, Elaine is fine.'

'Elaine, much as I applaud your intentions, we weren't necessarily going to take Emily away. It's not what we do unless it's unavoidable. Not that I want to prevent your sobriety,' Sally quickly added, 'but perhaps if we can, in the light of today's discussion, arrange a series of visits, in a supportive capacity, we will be able to forestall the need for any precipitate action which would likely upset both you and Emily. Do you have employment?'

Elaine paused briefly. 'Actually, I'm a solicitor, or, that is I was. I've got to renew my subscriptions to the Law Society so as to be registered again, then I'll work part time.'

'Really? Which field?' Sally was genuinely interested, but hoping it wouldn't be Family Law or anything related to Child Care.

'Medical Negligence. Usually on the side of the Provider as opposed to the Patient.' She looked every inch the corporate lawyer today, Sally thought.

'Can I arrange to come and see you next week, then? What I'd propose is that I complete an assessment over seven weeks and then see how we go from there. I'll need to talk to Emily as part of it and contact the school, your GP and anyone else involved. How does that sound?'

'Actually, I'd welcome that. It'll give me the chance to have a clean bill of health, so to speak. Tuesday would be particularly good for me.' Elaine was telling the truth and planned to attend an Alcoholics Anonymous meeting on Monday.

'Fine. Say one o'clock for two hours?'

'Thanks.'

Elaine got up to leave and Sally stood to open the door for her. She offered Elaine her hand to shake and was surprised when Elaine put her arms around her. While hugging her briefly, she whispered in Sally's ear, 'Thanks,' and left.

As Sally arrived back in the team room, Tom passed her a cup of tea.

'You'll need this. That won't have been easy.'

'Actually, it went rather well. I think I'll enjoy working with her.' Sally didn't elaborate as she turned towards Frances' office to confirm her decision to undertake a core assessment.

Geraldine Saunders had cut the fillet steak into strips. The onions and chestnut mushrooms were warming in the oven and she was adding lemon juice to the cream to finish her Beef Stroganoff. In the fridge she had smoked salmon and cream cheese parcels as a starter and Viennese curd cake with sour cherries as a dessert. The preparation had taken her all afternoon and she wanted everything just perfect for when Sally arrived home. Geraldine had come a long way during the last year; she had left Jake, kind, hard-working and affectionate Jake and fallen in love with Sally. The problem was that Sally and Jake worked in the same office and it wasn't easy for Sally to keep the fact that she was a gay woman concealed. Geraldine also had changed careers. She'd learned from Sally that you can separate your real self from your working self and she'd become a high-flying saleswoman, selling Chryslers for a living. Initially, it hadn't been easy dressing in a business suit and putting on her sales personality to spend her day flirting with all the men who were considering buying cars, but she'd become used to it. Now her sales figures were the best in the company and her commission made her better off than she'd ever been. And with Sally's social worker income, they were comfortable. Sally was wonderful; she was pretty, sexy, clever and she'd helped Geraldine to understand that it's more than okay to be gay. You don't have to look like a stereotypical lesbian with a political T-shirt. You can be yourself. Your real self. She reflected that life was good and she had a lot to be thankful for.

As she heard Sally's key in the door, she opened a bottle of Chilean Merlot and lit two red candles. 'Good day, my love?' she called.

'Not bad. Christine's got it on her again. I don't know how, but I get the distinct impression she knows about us.' Sally put down her work bag and slumped in an armchair in the front room.

'I've got a surprise and a possible solution. Come through.'

Sally walked through and her face lit up as she saw the dinner table with candles alight and the salmon parcels in place. 'When did you find the time to do all this?' She threw her arms around Geraldine and kissed her on the lips.'

Geraldine beamed. 'I took the afternoon off work specially to prepare it. It's a special occasion.'

'What have I forgotten?' Sally was concerned.

'Nothing. You've yet to find out what the occasion is. Sit down and start.'

Sally was hungry and she tucked in, savouring the smoked salmon and cream cheese. 'Go on then, put me out of my suspense.'

'You've been fabulous to me. I couldn't be more in love, but I do worry about you.'

'How?'

'Let me go on. It's a bit of a bum-clencher for me, this. As I was saying, you've helped me more than you'll ever know. You brought out the real me and turned my life around. It's different for you. You've always known about your sexuality. I didn't. I had unfulfilling relationships with men for years. Since we've been together, I've also found out that I have a whole other life. My job's great. Our home's perfect. I think about you all the time and feel not only safe, but invulnerable. What I'm working round to saying and I was going to wait until the dessert to ask, is shall we tie the knot? Civil ceremony and all that? I know what I want and I hope you want the same. Before you answer, I'll get the main course. It's one of your favourites. Think of it as bribery.' Gerry was fairly sure of what Sally's answer would be. They were both very much in love.

She carried out the dirty plates and put Beef Stroganoff on Basmati rice in front of Sally, then poured her a glass of the Merlot. 'That to your liking?'

'Bloody hell. You've pushed the boat out. Yes. Of course, angel. I'd love to get hitched.' Sally savoured the delicate taste of the tender beef in sour cream and drifted off in thought.

Sylvia (as she was originally named) Beckett had spent years avoiding talking about her sexual orientation. She'd been gay or heading that way as long as she could remember. As a little girl, she'd spent her time wanting to play with soldiers, cars and marbles rather than dolls. All her close friends had been boys. She'd accepted invitations at fifteen to go on dates with boys, but kissing them somehow just didn't work. It wasn't pleasant and she hated them wanting to fumble and fiddle with her and touch her body. It was when she was sixteen that she first saw a five-year old copy of the magazine Spare Rib. It wasn't like the Good Housekeeping or knitting magazines that were usually sold for women. It questioned whether the treatment of women was right. More importantly for her, it told her that it was possible for a woman to be attracted to women and she realised this was her. Try as she might, she could not find another copy, as its publication had stopped in 1993. Times were not easy at school or college after that, as she became known for rejecting advances by men. Nobody actually accused her of being a lesbian to her face and she didn't at that time have any steady relationships. She was a good-looking young woman and maintained the pretence that she had a boyfriend in America to whom she would remain faithful. She dressed carefully in as girly a way as she could so as to support her story. She tended to get away with it. She also learned to maintain relationships with men so as to be unavailable but not unfriendly.

Nobody could have been closer to another human being than Sally felt to Gerry. She had absolutely no doubt that she would love to commit to a civil ceremony. It would mean, she thought on reflection, that she would have to come clean about the nature of her relationship with Gerry. She would have to think about how to do that at work, particularly as Gerry had been Jake's partner and he didn't know that the Sylvia she'd left him for was in fact none other than Sally Beckett. She thought that Chrissie at work must know. She'd been very uncommunicative and cold of late. If she came out, it probably wouldn't make things worse. Supposing she invited her team to the civil ceremony? That way she'd know who felt uncomfortable. She'd think it through and pick her time.

The sour cherries were singularly good with the curd cake. A commitment had been made and both were delighted with the decision. It really was a special occasion.

# Chapter Ten

'Get away from my house. I don't care what excuses you have. I won't forgive you for what you did to me. But you start threatening my son in any way and even that pales into insignificance. Get out.' Voice raised. 'Fuck off.'

'But Lakhi, my love, my betrothed, I really don't know what you are referring to. I would never do anything to harm you or Nikhil. He is like a son to me. I have no idea what you're talking about,' Naren protested.

It was Tuesday. Naren had arrived and knocked at the front door as Lakshmi was checking her emails. She had just read one from her telephone service provider, which she did not understand, as it offered her the new password she had requested to access her account. The thing was she hadn't requested a new password. As she realised it must be someone else who had requested it, it dawned on her that the harassment was even more wide-ranging than she had realised. And then she heard a knock on the door and had a sinking feeling that it might be him. She had quickly logged off and gone to challenge him about the letter and calls to the school. She had to admit, his denial was very persuasive. Then she thought about the Court transcript and remembered the rape. She was determined to see it through.

'Out now, or I call the Police.'

Naren went without argument, quietly stopping to say, 'You'll regret this.' Lakshmi telephoned the local locksmith to get the door locks changed for more secure ones.

As she returned to her computer, the doorbell rang. It surely couldn't be the locksmith so quickly and Naren had better not have come back. She was surprised to see Tom Davey standing at her door.

'Tom. Come in. Drink?'

'Thanks. Tea. Milk and two sugars.'

As she handed him a mug of tea, he began, 'You're a union member who's been suspended. You haven't approached us for help, so I thought I'd visit to see if you wanted support or representation.'

Lakshmi outlined her story to Tom, suggesting that she was being harassed by a former temporary partner, but not giving him much detail. Tom thought about the information briefly.

'I could try and negotiate you a decent reference. Once those audit boys get their teeth into you, you normally don't have a chance. If it were me I'd resign. They wouldn't have started it unless they had something pretty concrete to go on.'

Lakshmi's shock must have shown on her face. 'I'll tell you what. Let me give it some thought and I'll get back to you.' She stood up, pointedly as if to open the door for him on his way out.

Tom, almost involuntarily, got up to leave, 'Right then. You know where I am,' as she closed the front door with almost indecent haste behind him. She didn't want him to see her cry.

Back at the computer, without thinking why, she turned to her MSN profile. She was horrified to find a picture of herself naked with her legs open where she had placed a well-chosen head and shoulders photo taken several months before. Her shock and embarrassment turned to rage as she reached for the telephone directory to ring the police. On second thoughts, having remembered the password email, she decided against telephoning.

Twenty minutes later, eyes dried, she arrived at Jake's front door. She uncomfortably sat in his lounge and told him about the rape, the photograph, the school discussion and other details she'd not been able to tell him before.

'It's another grievance.' Jake disappeared to his bedroom and returned with a laptop, which he plugged in. A half hour later, they had between them written a grievance.

The Chief Executive

Dear Sir,

*I am in the unfortunate position of needing to submit a serious grievance. The circumstances are as follows.*

*From July this year I was the subject of an audit investigation by the Council which is still ongoing. The circumstances are not relevant as this grievance is not about the investigation as such, but the existence of the investigation is vital as background. I was suspended in June pending an investigation. In January I had met by what seemed chance at the time a man named Naren Bhargava. He appeared familiar with my work situation before I briefed him, but as I was very vulnerable I trusted him, felt isolated and temporarily developed a dependence on him. From the start of this relationship, Mr Bhargava appeared to have an uncanny knowledge of Council business insofar as it affected me. It is my impression that clearly he was either connected to the Council or someone within the Council was feeding him information about me.*

*During the audit investigation he told me details of the processes they were undertaking to the extent that he accurately predicted verbatim the communication they were due to send and took £1000 from me against my will on the basis that he was buying off the audit investigation, which I would never have approved of.*

*He came to my house and hit me and raped me citing matters he can only have known about from the audit investigators. He also said he had a meeting with the audit department and said he could get rid of all the work issues on receipt of £25,000 from me which he would pass to Council officers. I refused, as I know myself to be innocent on all counts and will not be part of any corrupt practices.*

*To date, I have suffered theft, rape and physical assault as a result of information the perpetrator of these acts has gained from the Council. I hold the Council vicariously liable for breach of confidentiality putting me at risk and causing me harm.*

*I will supply further information as required.*
*Yours faithfully,*
*Lakshmi Patel*

Thanking Jake, she took the letter to the Council offices and drove from there to the Police station. She was not aware of it, but she would be there for the next eight hours, apart from an accompanied break to go home and make sure Nikhil was okay and fed. She told them everything. She told them about the photographs, the theft, the offer to bribe the Council officers, the rape because of the CV and the unexplained illness. She told them she knew about the Court transcript and about her fears of being in trouble for fraud. She also told them about the letter and phone calls to the school and the email from her telephone service provider. She left nothing out. The Police officers, supportive and female, took her seriously and taped everything. She even told them about and showed them her grievance for vicarious liability. The Police wanted to hear it all. They called in a medical officer, who took a hair sample and a blood test. It was clear that they already knew some details about Naren Bhargava and wanted all the information she could give. As she related it, Lakshmi cried. When she left, she was so worn out she could barely remember her way home.

Two days later in the afternoon, Duncan Rheiner, the Council Deputy Chief Executive pushed a document across the table to John Knight.

'You're the audit investigator. How did you recruit that informant?'

'Bhargava? I met him in a pub. When I told him I worked for the Council, he asked if I had anything to do with fraud in benefits. I told him I knew someone who did and he asked what a member of the public should do with information that the Council needed. He then gave me his name and made an appointment to meet with me promising he could help me. It was almost, thinking back, as if he knew about our arrangement. We must have had about five meetings before he asked whether I was interested in a private arrangement for him to gather information and it went from there. He said when we eventually made an arrangement that he would find interviewees and offer them a settlement without any link ever being made to me or the Council. I told him I would deny any knowledge if any of it came to light. As you know, we've only ever used informants for these arrangements five times or so each.'

Duncan listened carefully. 'And did you make checks?'

John nodded. 'He and his wife are between them paying Council Tax on three of our properties, though he's supposedly got three others. No apparent debts and no other concerns I could detect. Not an undercover police officer or investigator, although I couldn't find out much about his past. Says he's in import/export and spends a lot of time abroad, particularly in India. As for the target, she's got about thirty-six thousand pounds in savings and her family is up north and in London with various businesses. Good target. Son at private Hindu school and not a lot of support. Employed by us as a social worker. Seemed ideal.'

Duncan and John had had many such conversations in the past. They had discovered an excellent money making scheme some fifteen years prior in which they would find and investigate a vulnerable employee and recruit a third party to befriend their victim. When there looked like a possibility of a dismissal, the third person would then 'represent' the target in a private capacity on a conditional fee basis, along the lines of an exoneration being worth five thousand pounds, a formal warning worth two thousand pounds and a dismissal worth nothing at all. The fee would be split. As long as they stayed within the Asian community and Duncan heard the case, it had been foolproof. The 'fee' was split between the three of them. The difficulty they faced now was that John's new recruit had run his own agenda, saying he could get five times the normal figure. Now they had had a grievance from the victim and discovered that their man had misused the information they had allowed him to have. Even worse, the Chief Executive had seen the allegations.

'I'll resolve it by investigating the grievance myself and scaring her into withdrawing it.' Duncan Rheiner, a man of considerable talent, charm and power might normally have succeeded, but had not taken account of either Lakshmi's new-found self-confidence, or Jake, her researcher behind the scenes. It was going to cost both Duncan and John dearly.

# Eleven

Megasave has a particularly good fish counter. Jake was looking at the monkfish, when he spotted four lemon sole fillets reduced to half price.

'Those'll do nicely,' he smiled at the young woman in a netted hat.

'I had my eye on those.' The slightly husky voice with a smile in it came from behind Jake. He turned, to see a woman with strawberry blond hair falling Lauren Bacall-style in long natural curls onto her shoulders and a straight-toothed very pleasant smile. He noticed in a glance that her five-foot eight frame was nicely curvy and she was dressed in an elegant casual grey suit.

'You can have them if you like,' he said, 'or two of them, as you wish.' Then, chancing his arm, 'Or we could barter over a cup of coffee in the café in the corner.'

'Deal.' And a gentle laugh followed it. 'Barter and coffee it is.'

Over cappuccinos and double espressos, Jake found out that Joanne Cooke was thirty-four, twice-divorced, with a fourteen year old daughter called Amy. He also discovered that she'd given up on men and decided she was quite the most attractive woman he'd ever met. Joanne, for her part, was surprised at herself. She wouldn't normally initiate a discussion with a strange man anywhere, especially in the supermarket. She'd surreptitiously checked the contents of his shopping trolley; smoked salmon, expensive ground Fairtrade coffee, sugar-free muesli, skimmed milk, lager, steak and vegetables. Probably various other things she'd missed. He had a diet of someone who was healthy and not short of money. Twin pack of quilted toilet rolls and no ring or ring marks. Clean nails. Single then. Casual clothing, but well-dressed. Nice chukka boots. Good taste, but hetero. And a sad look in those blue eyes. Unusual, blue eyes on someone so dark-haired. Easy smile and clean-shaven. Educated accent, no obvious tattoos, jewellery or piercings. All boxes ticked and a lovely direct manner to polish it off. They were in the café for just over two hours, four cappuccinos and four double espressos. Neither really wanted the conversation to end. They brokered a sensible deal that Jake would keep the fish and cook them in Vermouth. Joanne would come round on Saturday and share them with him. By the time they left Megasave, Jake knew that Joanne lived on the Derbyshire-Staffordshire border in a two-acre smallholding with 14-year old daughter Amy, a scraggy dog called Moppet and a hamster called Gizmo. He also knew that she regarded social workers as dysfunctional busybodies, based on two sandal wearers with disruptive children who had been her neighbours when she had lived in Wombwell. Jake very much hoped he could persuade her that there was an alternative view. Joanne was surprised to learn he was a social worker. No beard, no sandals and a nice fresh cleanness about him. If he didn't fit the stereotype, she might have half an interest.

She was still surprised, as she got into her ancient 230 SL Mercedes that she had agreed to have dinner with him on Saturday.

Thirteen weeks to the day since he had last been there, Jake drove his Peugeot into his office car park. He sat for five minutes, waiting for the sick feeling to subside before undoing his seatbelt and walking through the front door.

'Jake,' Sue smiled warmly, 'nice to see you back.' She meant it. Word had even reached the reception desk that Jake was suspended. Nobody would tell her what for, but she knew without question that it could not have been for anything fraudulent or sexually related. She doubted it was for him doing anything wrong in professional terms, so assumed Jake was being scapegoated for the Hegarty twin's death. Everyone knew Frances hated him. Everyone also knew he'd come back off suspension because they'd got it wrong.

Jake had received a phone call the previous Friday out of the blue from Frances Phillips, who'd come round to see him that same afternoon with Hilary Campbell. He'd been told that as a result of information received during the investigation process, the suspension was to be lifted. He was to come back to work during the following week and was not permitted to speak about the circumstances, the reasons or any other issues concerning his suspension to any of his colleagues.

He walked into the team room with some trepidation. At first it appeared to be entirely empty, which was unusual for ten-past eleven on a Monday morning. He'd just sat down at his desk when Frances' door opened and out walked his four remaining colleagues, each carrying a white cardboard box and cheering enthusiastically.

'Jake, these are to celebrate your return.' The cream cakes were placed on Lakshmi's empty desk and Frances put down cartons of grape juice to accompany them.

'And we're all delighted you're back. I'm speaking for all of us.' If Jake was surprised that the words had come from Frances, he was even more surprised to see that she, in common with Sally and Chrissie, appeared genuinely delighted. 'When we've done celebrating, perhaps we should have a supervision session, but there's no hurry. Let's savour the moment.'

'I'm not sure where to start.' It was 2.15 and Jake sat in Frances' office. 'Perhaps I should say I may have misjudged you and apologise for that. To bring you up to date, Lakshmi Patel and Alison Bryant are not at work. I'm afraid I can't give you details. I'd be in agreeance for you to presume where you left off.'

Some things don't change, Jake reflected. She's still massacring the English language. Jake was beginning to feel less anxious about being back. He wondered how much Frances knew about either Alison's or Lakshmi's situations. She certainly wouldn't realise how well briefed he was on Lakshmi's in particular.

'Now then. Curtis Wilson, now back at home. Assess first then close if appropriate. Daley Stevens. We have to find a way of getting him out of Beech Lodge. Sarah and Harley Moss. He's down in London in Great Ormond Street Hospital, but we really need to get him back up here, as he's taking up valuable bed space. They haven't found an explanation for his blue fits and to be honest, she won't communicate with Chrissie McBride. Would you mind having the case back?'

Jake had given Sarah and Harley a great deal of thought while he had been off. Usually in the early hours of the morning, after he had woken with thoughts of Ricky Hegarty's death.

'I suppose Fictitious or Fabricated Illness Syndrome, as they call Munchausen's Syndrome by Proxy nowadays has been explored and ruled out?'

'Shit.'

'Frances, I'm the one that swears, remember?' Jake had quick verbal reflexes.

Frances went a deep red colour, 'Okay, I was out of order when I told you off and I apologise. But you repeat that to a living soul and I'll deny it and give you a hard time for the rest of your natural life. New start?'

'I'll think about it. I've thought about it. New start.'

'No more mention of it. That's a management instruction.'

Frances was temporarily lost in thought; she could find him a valuable team member. He was honest and dependable. 'I just realised that I should have considered MSbP a possibility. I'm not sure where the Authority or even the theory stands nowadays on induced illness. Is it still regarded as a Syndrome? Does anyone know what are the explanations for it? I'm afraid I don't. What's your view as to how to proceed?'

Between them, until four o'clock, they worked out a tentative strategy. Whatever the potential cause or explanation for Sarah's possible treatment of baby Harley, they decided they could not take the risk of doing nothing. The difficulty was that there was no evidence and it was therefore unlikely that the Police would be able to take any action. It also called into question whether an Emergency Protection Order could be gained to remove him from his mother. It was, they agreed, worth trying. It would be a potential serious risk to

Harley if the fits had been induced. They would hopefully plan to place him long-term with his grandparents anyway, who were to be contacted first by Jake. Sarah and Harley would be brought back from London and Frances would authorise Jake to apply for an Emergency Protection Order, Jake would ring Legal and start Care Proceedings and he would then ring Fostering to get a placement for Harley.

'Bear with me. Transferring.' Greensleeves on Stylophone. Again. Jake was waiting for Fostering Section. Eventually, 'Dee Smith 'ere. I 'ope you're not after a placement.'

'Two, actually.' A long pause and mechanic-type sucking noises over the telephone.

Eventually, 'Go on, then.' Jake first patiently explained Daley's position, emphasising his ethnic origin and the fact that his identity needs would have to be recognised to be addressed.

'You found me somewhere for him last time I enquired.'

'And that was?'

'Four months ago or thereabouts.'

'Yer 'evin a larf. And the other?'

Jake described Harley, emphasising the planned short-term nature of the prospective placement.

'Leave that one with me. I might be able to do something with one under a year old.' Dee put down the telephone.

Time to look more imaginatively at how to place Daley. Jacob knew a number of families whose children had grown up, or who didn't have children who would love to foster, but wouldn't be willing to go through the rigmarole of being assessed. This was as often as not because they just didn't trust social workers. Thinking about trustworthy people who were not enamoured of social workers, he had an idea.

On the other end of the telephone, a friendly voice picked up. 'Joanne Cooke.'

'It's Jacob Atkinson from Social Services. Can I pick your brains?'

'You're being very formal, love. This is obviously business.'

And switching to a mock business voice, 'How may I help you?' The tone raised, Australian-style at the end of the question.

Jake and Joanne had been seeing each other for a few weeks. By now Jake was quite sure he had never met anyone so perfect. Joanne was wondering whether she might consider a permanent relationship. Again. Third time lucky perhaps, or maybe hope over experience. Jake told her in a half-whisper that he was looking for someone who would like to foster and that he thought he might know a way to short-circuit the process. He wanted it for a nice, artistic fifteen year old of dual heritage, West Indian and English. A seriously nice lad, although he couldn't guarantee there would never be teenage tantrums. But it had to be someone special.

'Just a minute. I need to close my door.' Joanne's job in Derby Council as Human Resources and Non Vocational Qualification Verifier/Assessor was a tough one, made more difficult by her manager Sandra's bullying attitude. There was never a chance of doing anything about it, because Sandra regularly exchanged bodily fluids with the Chief Executive, who protected her. Sandra's husband, Paul, a fireman, had no idea. But if Joanne was overheard on non-work business, Sandra may well give her a hard time.

Joanne was surprisingly quick in her response to Jake's question. 'I've got a cousin, Linda, who lives in Sandiacre. She left it too late to have children, but I can tell you she's brilliant, especially with teenagers, has spoken about fostering for years and, incidentally is married to Charles. He's black, American and the world's best role model. And he's a professional sculptor. Any good?'

Jake couldn't believe it. 'Can you sound her out? If she's interested, I'll introduce her as a social aunt to the lad. She can take him out as many times as she wants and we can see if they like each other. We'll need a Criminal Records Bureau check on them both first, which can take anything from two to ten weeks. Then if she's interested, we can see if it's a runner. Could there be any problems with a CRB check?'

Joanne laughed. 'I don't think so. She's a policewoman.'

It was a week later, as Jake put the telephone down, having spoken to Linda Carter, that Sally Beckett approached him. 'Chrissie and I are not happy. You're cheating Reg 38 to engineer a Friends and Family fostering setup. We don't think you can do that.'

'Pick it up with Frances. She's aware,' Jake replied.

'We did and she practically threw us out of her office.'

It's a tricky question as to whether you do whatever it takes to advance the welfare of the people you are there to help, or whether you do everything the conventional way. Jake knew the odds on Daley ever being found a foster carer through fostering were limited. If he did, the odds on it being perfect were low. Under Regulation 38 of the Fostering Regulations 2002, a child could be placed with family or friends on an immediate basis for up to six weeks. If they were assessed by Fostering Section within those six weeks, the child could stay for up to six months. Within those six months there could be a full fostering assessment with that specific child in mind to enable a permanent or semi permanent placement. Jake's plan was to introduce Linda and Charles Carter as a Social Aunt and Uncle and if they liked Daley, for them to apply to have him placed with them under Regulation 38 on the basis they fitted the criteria of friends or family. They could then go through the child-specific assessment.

Linda had apologised for having the same name as the actress who had been Wonder Woman and was not particularly concerned that the Local Authority would not necessarily pay as much under Regulation 38 as they would pay to conventionally approved foster carers.

It would work far better than any of them imagined. In years to come, Jake and Joanne would be given a picture from Daley Stevens' Graduation Exhibition from the Slade School of Fine Art in London. But Jake could not have foreseen it at the time. Neither could he have foreseen that that oil painting, entitled 'Nude with Roses' would come to be worth thousands.

Monica was sitting in Jake's lounge. Unusually, she was there without breaching Council rules, as Jake was no longer suspended.

'So, tell me straight. Nobody comes out of a suspension without serious emotional damage. How are you? I want to know the truth warts and all. You're such a kind man, you've put all that energy into caring about Lakshmi and I want to know about you.'

Jake knew he could not pull a fast one past Monnie. 'It's been a lot easier since I met Joanne.'

'But what I want to know is that she's good to you. You're always giving and never taking time for yourself. You're a deep one and there's something you've not shared. Some days, you look haunted. Now this old woman knows it's not the suspension, because it's over. You're not getting a hard time from Frances, because she's now decided you're the couils de chien.'

'The what?' Jake interrupted.

'Dog's bollocks. Couils. Bollocks in French.' Without pausing, 'So what is it? And while I'm at it I want to know about your new love interest, no holes barred, except… well you can bar certain holes.' Jake was honest and open about waking most nights thinking about Ricky. He told her about the nightmares where he saw Ricky fall and didn't catch him and watched his little body break on the concrete. How he imagined the beautiful big eyes glazed-over in death. Tears ran down his face as he sat in silence.

'And Joanne?' Jake told of their meeting. He spoke of his visits to her place, with its driveway snaking lazily round the farmhouse and its carefully cultivated allotment containing raspberries, strawberries, peas, Black Aztec sweet corn, kohl rabi and Jersey Royals. He spoke about Amy, with her healthy teenage curiosity, her quick sense of humour and utter devotion to her mother. He spoke about the old Mercedes sports car that spent as much time in the garage as on the road. He told her about Joanne, who refused to be a trophy wife, eye candy to her two previous husbands, both of whom had been lawyers, the first a physically abusive barrister and the second an emotionally abusive and philandering solicitor. He spoke about her gentle affectionate nature and deep infectious laugh.

'So you're really smitten, then?'

'I would be, but she hates social workers. And I can't help but feel that as soon as she gets to know me properly, you won't see her for dust.'

'Stupid bastard, if it wasn't for the fact that you're thirty years too young, I'd push Pat over a cliff and have you myself. Don't you ever think you're not good enough for anyone.'

'Anyway,' continued Jake, changing the subject, 'what happened to the woman who had to be taught to say, 'Ça suffit?' before she took a trip to France? You're suddenly dropping French phrases into your conversation.'

'Well that's different. I've a PhD in profanity. It's my version of Talking in Tongues. Ever since Pat gave me a Miraculous Medal when I was about your age, I've had this remarkable talent. I think of it as the gift of Divine Interjection. The Gift of the Gob. But as you asked, your phrase was a miracle in itself. I went to the supermarket in Champagne where I was staying. It's a fuck-off place, that supermarket. You need a Sat Nav once you're inside. Anyway, I wheeled up my trolley full of red wine and bubbly and avoided getting run over by the girls on skates. I smiled my best French smile, held up my credit card and said, 'Ça suffit?' and the woman gabbled at me for twenty minutes. We had a rare conversation.'

'So you understood her?'

'Not a feckin' syllable, but I smiled and nodded, concluded our business and I don't think she was any the wiser. But I do love it over there.' Jake pictured it. He could just see Monnie doing that. And a slow smile spread from his mouth to his eyes.

Monica stood up to go. 'Will you do me a favour?'

'Of course.'

'For the sake of the good Lord and all your friends and clients, ask your doctor to refer you for counselling. You need to exorcise your ghosts.'

## Twelve

Tom and Lakshmi sat opposite each other in Lakshmi's front room, Lakshmi cross-legged on the floor and Tom on a two-seater sofa. Lakshmi had meditated and prayed for three hours early that morning in the same position she was in now.

She glared at Tom. 'What do you mean, you're dropping my case?'

'Nobody has ever put in a grievance about the Chief Executive before. You haven't said what he has done, so you can't possibly get anywhere with it. I'm not sure what you mean by vicarious liability and I can't see what you hope to get out of it.'

'Well,' Lakshmi said quietly, 'I've got an investigation meeting on Wednesday. I understand what I'm doing with it. I'm seeing the Assistant Chief Executive, Duncan Rheiner. I'll handle it myself.'

'I'll accompany you for support, but I'm not representing you.'

Tom was stuck. He couldn't be seen to be a troublemaker in front of such senior staff. But he had to know what was going on. He'd been interviewed by the Head of Audit, who had pushed him very hard to know what evidence Lakshmi had and whether she had involved the Police. Tom didn't know and told them so. Having been assured that they would be grateful at the highest level to know, Tom promised to find out what he could. They had stressed it. Very Grateful. It was clear to Tom that Lakshmi was doing something very wrong. He didn't know what it was, but he couldn't afford to be implicated. He would speak to Lakshmi beforehand and to Mr Rheiner after the Wednesday meeting. He was meeting Lakshmi at nine prior to the ten-thirty meeting. He would be prepared.

At nine o'clock prompt on Wednesday, the doorbell of the union office rang and Tom pressed the intercom button to let Lakshmi in. He was surprised that the Lakshmi who came in was not the Lakshmi he knew. Wearing a very well-tailored business suit, high heels and skilfully applied make-up, she swept in.

'You look nice.'

Lakshmi gave a withering smile. 'Thanks.' No explanation.

Tom was hesitant, beginning, 'If I'm to represent you adequately, I need to know what your evidence is for your allegations.'

'You're not representing me. You said so.' Lakshmi appeared focused, very confident and calmer than anyone he had ever seen prior to so formal an interview.

'You do understand the seriousness of this interview?'

'Yes. Do you?'

'I presume you've got evidence?'

'Yes.' She was carrying a soft leather briefcase.

He'd worked in the same team as her and never seen this side of her character. He was reminded of the calm authority of Kam Kaur, the Police officer he'd worked with. Suddenly Tom was worried. He had the uncomfortable impression that there could be something bigger happening here than he knew about.

'Have you, er, reported your concerns to the Police?' Nervously.

'And of what concern would it be? Even if you were representing me, which you're not, I fail to see what relevance it has to the union.' God, she sounds like a lawyer, he thought. It was a very uncomfortable ninety minutes for Tom. Lakshmi, on the other hand, did not change her demeanour.

At ten-thirty exactly, they were welcomed into Duncan Rheiner's office.

'Coffee, tea, soft drink?'

Both accepted a cup of tea, which was brought in with a plate of assorted biscuits. Lakshmi was surprised at the treatment she was getting. Tom was also. He had never heard of any hearing or investigation meeting where the member of staff was offered biscuits.

'Let's try and do this in as civilised a way as we can.' Duncan was a handsome man in his forties, with a London accent and a lean appearance. He had well cut straight almost white hair and the obligatory striped shirt, with a diagonally striped tie. Probably public school, gentlemen's club or regimental was Tom's view. He also had an easy smile and deep, piercing blue eyes. 'Well, I've read your letter. These are serious matters and we take them seriously. First, let me ask who you consider may be responsible for the Council acts you intimate in your letter. It appears to be a variety of breaches of confidential information.'

Lakshmi answered, without a flicker, 'I have no single individual to name. The basis of my complaint is that the various pieces of information have been leaked. Even if the leak is eventually found to be anonymous, the Council is still liable if the leak can be shown to have happened. That I have been assaulted I can offer evidence, as I went to my GP and I will happily give permission for my medical records to be accessed. That the Audit Department has communicated with Mr Bhargava is something you can to establish with them.

There is a link between the actions taken by him and the information given to him.'

'Are you saying it was the audit department?' Duncan suddenly and fleetingly had an eager look in his deep blue eyes.'

'It is based on information known only to the audit department. It could be a clerk or an admin officer. It could be a cleaner. It could be any one of their professional staff. It could be a secretary. It could be you. You are investigating. First establish that there is a link between Bhargava and the Council, then look for the leak.'

'Why, to ask bluntly, should I believe that this man, who I presume actually exists, should not legitimately be helping our audit department with its enquiries? And why should I not just contact him and ask?'

Lakshmi noticed that Duncan had gone slightly red and had not asked any of Naren's contact details.

'Because he is a dangerous man.' Lakshmi said, calmly and quietly. And from her soft brown case, she removed a Court transcript photocopy and passed it across the oak table at which they were sitting.

Duncan Rheiner looked at it as if to skim read it, then changed his mind. He read it carefully and then read it again. Very red-faced and with a look of fury across his face, he asked very calmly, 'And have you shared your concerns with the Police?'

'I'm sorry, but I don't think that's any business of the Council's.' Lakshmi looked Duncan straight in the eye.

He shifted uncomfortably in his chair and briefly looked at Tom, 'Well we need to know if they are interested. Have you done a video interview?' And turning to Tom, he said, still sounding very calm, but looking anything but calm, 'As her representative, I'm sure you can enlighten us on this.'

Before Tom could say anything, Lakshmi replied 'Actually Tom is not my representative. He is here merely to support me. Let me give you a clear answer to your question. I am not going to tell you. So there is no point in asking further about that. In fact I don't think there is any further information with which I can help you. Good day.'

She stood up, fastened her suit jacket and walked to the door. As she opened it, she turned round. 'Thank you for the tea.' And left.

Tom scurried out after her. 'What the hell were you thinking? Nobody speaks to Mr Rheiner like that.'

'Wrong, Tom.' Lakshmi smiled, reflecting an inner tranquillity, 'I do.'

Detective Constable Stephanie Johanssen was waiting outside Lakshmi's house in a Vauxhall Astra without wheel trims when Lakshmi returned home.

She sat in Lakshmi's front room. 'There are two things I have to say to you. The first is that the test for poison carried out by our Medical Officer indicates some presence of arsenic in your system. The second is I have to ask you whether and when you are next being interviewed by your employers.' Lakshmi explained that was where she had just come from.

'What did you say about your involvement with us?' Stephanie looked serious.

'I told them it had nothing to do with the Council whether or not I was in touch with the Police. They did ask, several times.'

Stephanie looked relieved. 'Thank goodness. Under no circumstances should you tell them anything of your involvement with us. Is that understood?'

'Sure.' Lakshmi was curious, but did not ask.

DC Johanssen thanked Lakshmi for her time and left. She was on her way to arrest Naren Bhargava. She wanted him put away for good. She had enlisted, with the permission of her Superintendent, her colleague and friend Kam Kaur from the Child Protection Unit. They both knew that Naren Bhargava, an Indian Hindu male, would resent being arrested by Kamalgit Kaur, an Indian Sikh female. From his perspective, women, especially Indian women should not ever challenge or disrespect the actions or views of a man. Within a few days, she and her colleagues planned to arrest several Council Officers, partly depending on what names they were given by Naren Bhargava. What Lakshmi did not know was that she was the most significant of four current victims whose statements had enabled this major action. Neither did she know that the Police had been watching elements of the Council where they suspected serious corruption, or that Naren was a recently recruited agent in a well-established scam. The Police suspected that it was an extremely senior official who was masterminding it and thought it likely that over the years, several thousands of pounds had been paid by employees desperate not to be dismissed and, as they thought, imprisoned.

Jake walked up the stone steps into the Court building. He was recognised by the Court administrative staff as he went to stand in line with the fine-payers and he was ushered through a side door into the office behind the glass partition.

'It's an Emergency Protection Order you phoned about, isn't it Mr Atkinson? Mr Bickley will see you in the Magistrates' retiring room.'

Jake smiled. 'I thought it might be Mr Wheeler,' relieved that it wasn't. He was sure Mr Wheeler didn't like him. He was surprised to be told that Mr Wheeler no longer sat as a Magistrate. He didn't ask. He had filled in the forms carefully, but was aware that there was plenty of scope for them to turn down this particular application. There wasn't an injury as such and no positive evidence that Harley's cyanotic episodes were caused by Sarah. Neither was it, in strict terms, an emergency. Sarah was being brought in an ambulance with Harley from Great Ormond Street to Northampton, where she would be met by Chrissie McBride and brought to the office. Her parents would be waiting in the office already aware that the child would be taken to temporary foster carers and they as grandparents would be assessed as potential safe carers for Harley. Care proceedings would be commenced in order that as carers they could be appropriately paid, or else it would only be minor expenses the Department could meet and they couldn't afford to do it on Child Benefit and Tax Credits alone. So the Emergency Protection Order was all important as part of the plan. If Jake's application was unsuccessful, he and Frances would have to rethink the whole thing.

Mr Bickley read the paperwork and signed the Order. Before Jake left, he said, 'Reading between the lines, I can see there are issues on which I could have questioned you. From what I know about your Department and what I've heard of you, it's not an action you will have taken without careful consideration. I wish you well.'

Jake thanked him, offering the deference due to a Justice of the Peace, took the Order and headed back to the office.

After a quick telephone call, Sarah was told her transport was now available and she and Harley were on their way to Northampton General Hospital. She had enjoyed her time in London and would miss Stringbean, whom she had been seeing for several weeks and with whom she had spent most nights during the past fortnight, but she liked the idea that she could continue her previous existence as the most heroic young mum on the planet.

Jacob Atkinson, Sally Beckett and Sarah's parents David and Susan Moss sat in the interview room, waiting. David and Susan had been briefed about the plan and had agreed to be assessed as prospective carers for Harley. Neither had shown a reaction when Jake had told them of his suspicions and his plan to take Harley from Sarah. Susan had said that it saddened her, but didn't surprise her. Sarah, an only child, had been unpredictable and out of control since she had been thirteen. Even when they bought her a kitten to try to enable the young Sarah to show responsibility, it had disappeared and Sarah had not seemed bothered. Her school had said that she had no friends and didn't contribute at all in class. She wasn't a stupid girl, but didn't apply herself at all. When she had been given straight Fs, failing all her General Certificate of Secondary Education exams, she didn't seem to care. She left school, left home, got pregnant with Liam virtually immediately and was given Council accommodation. She hadn't told anyone who was Liam's father. David had been more hurt than Susan when Liam had died of Sudden Infant Death Syndrome at just under three months. Whatever suffering Susan felt, she didn't show it. However, she was determined, along with David, to have, love and care for their grandson Harley.

Sarah was surprised to see her parents along with Jake and someone she did not know when Chrissie brought her into the interview room.

Chrissie handed a white envelope to Jake. 'Here's the Order. I didn't need to serve it.'

Jake took the Emergency Protection Order out of the envelope and everyone looked at him, expectantly.

'I don't know how much you've been told. As a Social Care Authority, we have some concerns over your possible care of Harley. There's no kind way of saying this. This,' and he held up the Court Order, 'authorises us to remove Harley from your care for up to seven days. Within that time, I shall be applying to the Court for a Care Order, which, if successful, will take some time to grant, but we hope to be allowed to care for Harley during that time. We have foster carers waiting to look after him, but in the long term it would be our plan that your parents here will eventually be able to look after Harley on a permanent basis. When you have finished with us, my advice is that you go and see a solicitor. Child Care Proceedings shouldn't cost you anything. However, I would really like it if you come with me to introduce Harley to the foster carers and meet them yourself.' He held the Order for Sarah to take.

Sarah, white as a sheet turned to Sally. 'Are you the boss? Which bastard is responsible for this?' Her fists were clenched tight and her knuckles were white.

Susan picked up Harley and initially sat him on her knee. She had tears streaming down her face and she lifted the child up to hug him tightly. Harley was silent. He was used to being cuddled by his grandmother and he obligingly put his little chubby arms round her neck.

Sally looked directly at Sarah. 'No, I'm not the boss, I'm a social worker same as Jake. It's Jake who's your social worker and he with whom you must discuss it.' Sarah let out a shriek as she stood up. She moved quickly across to Jake who was standing in an instant. She pummelled his upper chest with the side of her fists, sobbing as she did so. This time the tears were genuine.

'How could you? Bastard. I love that boy more than anything. No one'll take him from me.' She continued to pummel Jake as he backed out the door with her following, still hitting him. Detecting several people approaching, Jake held out his hands to gesture them to stay back, as Sarah ran out of energy and sat on the floor, curled up and sobbing.

Jake reached down to take her elbow and help her stand up. 'Shall we talk about it in the other room? You don't need the embarrassment of an audience.' He beckoned to Sally and the three of them went into a second interview room.

Jake signalled to Chrissie to ask if she would bring Sarah a cup of tea. An hour later, Jake, Sarah and Harley climbed into Jake's car, child seat already installed and went to take Harley to meet his new foster parents.

Sarah climbed out of the front seat of Jake's Peugeot and stood. She was numb. They really were taking Harley away. Harley, who she'd carried until he was born. She'd nurtured him on her own from a bald squinty little bundle to the beautiful tousle-haired blondie with chubby kissable cheeks and big blue eyes. It had been really hard work, especially for the first eight or nine weeks. She loved him so much, she didn't like to leave him with anyone. And now he was to be taken away from her and given to someone else. She couldn't understand why anyone would take him from her. She'd never hurt him. All she'd done was to prove to the world what a good mum she was. Sometimes you just have to show them the proof and that was all she'd done. She would never harm him. Without realising it, she was crying again.

Jake was now standing next to her with Harley in his arms. They were in front of a big house on an estate. One of those that was obviously originally a council house, but it was on a corner and was wider than it ought to be, There was a neatly-trimmed hedge and a people carrier in the driveway. Jake walked with her up to the white plastic front door and rang the bell.

'Jenny, I've brought you Harley. This is his mum, Sarah. I'm afraid I don't have much by way of clothes and equipment, but if we can't get them from home, we'll sort it out via requisitioning.'

Jenny Brinded held out her arms to take Harley, who obligingly held out his arms to be taken. 'He's lovely.' And turning to Sarah, 'We'll take good care of him while he's with us, don't you worry. He'll want for nothing.' Jenny ushered Jake and Sarah through the hallway into a large kitchen. It was modern and well-equipped with a wooden table and eight chairs around it. 'Cup of tea?'

Sarah looked at Jenny properly for the first time. She had a warm, motherly, smiley voice. Everything about her was round, from her shape to her glasses. She had an apron on.

Sarah didn't know what to say and Jake answered. 'Thanks. Lovely.'

Jenny passed Harley to Jake and attended to the kettle. She had an Aga cooker and lifted the lid to put the old whistling kettle onto it. It looked old-fashioned but very traditional to Sarah and it gave off a warmth she could feel from where she was standing. As they sat, a chocolate-coloured Labrador wandered through from what must have been the lounge. It sniffed at Jake then sniffed at Harley, before turning its attention to Sarah, wagging its tail.

'This is Mindy. She's lovely with children.' Jenny commented. Harley's face lit up as Mindy looked up to sniff at him, wagging her tail.

'Come to that, she's lovely with everyone. If ever we had burglars, she'd probably cover them with doggy kisses as they were leaving with a full swag bag.' Sarah gave a watery smile.

'How many others do you have at the moment?' Jake asked.

'Two. Brother and sister, Connor and Paige. Paige is eight and Connor six. They're at school at the moment, back at about ten to four. It's only two minutes' walk up the road. Then there's my own two Matthew and Claire. Matthew's seventeen and Claire fifteen. They're all looking forward to Harley's arrival.'

Mindy ambled over to the Aga and flopped down in front of it as Jenny put a plate of Fondant Fancies on the table, then a cup of tea in front of each of them.

'Help yourself to sugar and milk. And please have a cake. I've got cupboards full of cake and I'm supposed to be losing weight.' She lifted Harley back from Jake.

Sarah realised she was hungry and took a pink one. Jenny was nice and if she had been going to choose anyone to look after Harley it would have been someone like this.

Eventually, Jake stood up. 'I've got some paperwork for you to sign and I'm aware you're due to go and get Paige and Connor from school.' Sarah suddenly felt sick. She was going to have to leave Harley behind. No matter how nice this lady was, she couldn't live without him.

'Can I cuddle him before we leave?' Sarah's voice was almost a whisper. It was Jenny's turn to look upset. She gave Sarah a folded piece of paper.

'I'm not supposed to do this, but here's our phone number and my mobile. Ring any time you want to know how he's doing. And we'll see you at reviews and I'm sure Jake will arrange for you to have regular contact with him.' She handed Harley to Sarah. Sarah, with tears running silently down both cheeks, whispered to Harley, 'Mummy will love you forever.' She held him to her and hugged him, sniffing as if to remember his smell. After a few minutes of silence, she handed him back to Jenny.

Jake recognised the need to leave quickly and walked with Sarah to his car, signalling to Jenny to stay in the kitchen. Sarah walked out with dignity and a straight back. As Jake drove down the road, she burst into tears and cried inconsolably.

On the following Thursday, Sarah cashed her Child Benefit and caught a train to London. The Northern Line Underground to Camden Town was busy and she walked with some relief into Camden Market. Stringbean's stall was not there. She crossed the road to his flat and could get no answer. Looking through the letterbox, it looked deserted. She went back to the market to where his stall should have been.

'Hi, Sarah. Where you been?' It was Steve, with the stall next door.

'Hi Steve. Know where Stringbean went?'

'Didn't you hear? He's got one of Her Majesty's bedsits at Wormwood Scrubs.'

'Sorry?' Sarah had no idea what Steve meant.

'Arrested. Busted for dope. Sent down for two years. Thought you'd have known. He was sentenced last week. 'Scuse me I've got a customer.' When Steve turned back, Sarah was gone. So was her former existence.

# Thirteen

It was Saturday afternoon. Lakshmi was sitting in Jake's lounge opposite Jake and Joanne. Jake was reading a letter from the Council.

*Dear Ms Patel,*
*As a result of a combination of circumstances, there will be no further continuation of the previous audit investigation concerning you. We are most anxious to meet with you to discuss a satisfactory way forward. You are invited to attend a meeting this Friday at 2 o'clock. You may bring to this meeting a friend, colleague or representative of your choosing, but not a solicitor. This meeting will take place in my office and I would request that discretion be observed until we have spoken.*
*Yours sincerely,*
*Eric Sefton*
*Chief Executive*

'So they have decided not to proceed with your audit investigation. I can't understand why it's come from the Chief Executive, who's signed it himself. What are you going to do?' Jake was genuinely curious.

'Jake,' said Lakshmi quietly, 'my reason for bringing it to you is to ask you to be the one to accompany me. I don't know what he wants. You've got pretty good at employment law and I don't trust Tom or any of his union colleagues. Please will you do it?' Her voice had a note of desperation.

'I can only think he wants a compromise agreement. That's a process by which you agree to leave on a particular date, there is a confidentiality clause, they agree to pay you a sum of money and you ask for a decent reference. Has anything happened that you think might have affected the case that you know of?'

'Naren was arrested yesterday.' Lakshmi said. 'I meant to tell you, but it was just such a sense of relief, I sort of lost track of time. DC Johanssen told me I mustn't tell the Council about my involvement with the Police, so I wondered if she suspects the Council of something in connection with him.'

Jake smiled. 'So they need to gag you. If I've got an accurate measure of your case, it's a waste of time, because it'll probably be big news anyway. I'll come with you.' Then as an afterthought, 'If they were looking to buy you off, how much would you want?'

'I don't know. I suppose enough to tide me over to my next job. Say ten or fifteen thousand. Does that sound greedy?'

Jake thought about it. 'We'll see on Friday.'

The following Friday, two suited social workers were ushered into the Chief Executive's office, where the Corporate Head of Human Resources, Paula Browne, was sitting at a table with Eric Sefton, the Chief Executive.

Introductions over, Eric Sefton spoke. 'We are in a somewhat embarrassing position. If you are prepared to treat this conversation with absolute confidentiality, I will be open with you.' Both agreed, before Eric continued, 'There has been information about you passed to and from the Council by someone currently on remand and awaiting trial for fraud. Also on remand are certain of my staff. You made a claim to do with the Council's vicarious liability for certain disadvantage to which you were allegedly subjected. We do not wish to admit it, but equally do not wish to defend it. As a prospective way forward, we propose an agreement to enable your departure with dignity. Would you wish to consider leaving the Council if the conditions were right?'

Jake was quick in responding. 'Can we discuss it for a few minutes?'

'By all means. We anticipated that and have a room set aside for you. We'll look in, say, in a half hour?' Jake and Lakshmi nodded and the Chief Executive himself led them along a corridor to an office. On the table were sandwiches, tea, coffee, biscuits and cakes.

'Vegetarian, I'm told. Please help yourself. I'll see you in a half hour.'

Lakshmi sat down. 'Wow. What d'you think?'

'Cakes. Pretty impressive.'

'No, arsehole. About the amount they'll go to.'

'I think you've been learning from Monica. I also think we should make a cheeky request on the basis you've got to find another job. A year's salary maybe? That's twenty-eight thousand or thereabouts.'

Lakshmi looked, wide-eyed.

'Are you kidding? You can do the bloody talking. Usually I'll negotiate anything, but I feel a bit out of my depth here.'

'Go on, then. I'll do it. But if I screw it up I'm not taking the blame.'

'Have you had sufficient time to think?' Eric sat calmly. He would resolve this today. He had done his homework and knew what this woman would take, or so he thought. But the man, Atkinson? Seems smart in every way. He'd make sure his talents were well used once this was over.

Jake began, 'If it's allowed, sir, I'll do the talking.'

'Allowed? Of course. And it's Eric.'

'Well, Eric, from where Lakshmi stands, she's got to get another job. She's been subjected to a difficult set of circumstances in respect of the suspension alone. There are two cases that come to mind. One's called 'Mezey v South West London Hospitals Trust', which some see as defining suspension as not a neutral act. The other's Gogay v Hertfordshire County Council. We understand the Council does not want to accept vicarious liability, but are not sure what you do accept. If I said two years' salary by way of payment without prejudice, immediate agreed termination of contract, agreement to make no claim against the Council, a confidentiality clause and a good reference as Lakshmi has to find another job, how would you respond?'

'I've got an alternative proposal.' Eric smiled, calmly. This man was very good. Eric knew of Gogay but not Mezey. 'Reduce the figure to fifty thousand, we have a word with AWG, the Asian Women's Group, a social work project in the community that we fund. Its Assistant Director post is vacant and pays just over forty thousand a year. Your other suggestions stand and that improves the position for both sides.'

Back in the other room, Lakshmi turned to Jake. 'You cheeky bastard. You didn't tell me you were going to ask for two years. And where did all that technical stuff come from?'

'You can always let them barter you down, so you have to start high. But I didn't think he'd agree that figure that easily. And it's from Legal Action Group Guide to Employment Law, Selwyn's and the internet.

Anyway it's your choice. Deal or no deal? Ask the audience or phone a friend?'

'You watch too much TV. I've seen both those shows as well and dreamed about what if it was me getting the money and that's what it feels like now. Let's get back in there before he changes his mind.' Lakshmi was positively glowing.

Twenty minutes later, as Eric Sefton's office door closed behind Jake and Lakshmi, Eric turned to Paula. 'Can you find out about Jacob Atkinson for me, what he does, what his work record's like and so on? You know the form. And if possible, today, while I still remember? Oh and I trust you'll bring me whatever needs to be signed to sort out the Patel situation?'

'No problem, Eric. Give me an hour and I'll be back up; assuming you're free then.'

'An hour then. See you at about four-thirty.' Eric Sefton breathed a sigh of relief. Significantly more expensive than he had intended, but the Patel problem was resolved and that Atkinson was definitely worth making good use of.

'Spot on time as usual Paula. What have you got for me?'

Eric had spent much of the previous hour on the telephone to the Asian Women's Group. They had no obvious front runner for the vacant Assistant Director post. Eric had made it clear that in Lakshmi Patel he had an excellent candidate to personally recommend whose persuasive powers would increase the likelihood of success in applications to the Council for future funding.

Unsurprisingly, having applied for the Assistant Director post at AWG, Lakshmi Patel was successful and seamlessly moved into a career in management and bought herself a brand-new Volkswagen Golf Cabriolet.

Paula sat down. 'Jacob Atkinson. Temporary social worker. Qualified for two years. Good all-rounder. Apparently very bright, if a bit pedantic. Has picked up some employment law knowledge while recently suspended for three months. That suspension needs looking at, because it doesn't make sense to me.'

'In what way?'

'It seems that he made an allegation under the whistleblowing procedure that the head of one of our residential homes had sexually abused a child in our care.'

'I presume he was appropriately dealt with?' Eric was concerned. He'd already had one difficult situation with what looked like a nasty scam by Duncan, his deputy, the audit department and a shady member of the public. The Police were dealing with them and it looked as if Duncan and others might serve a term in prison. He hadn't yet had to face the publicity that would generate, or the possible claims from previous targets of this unpleasant little group. He didn't want another scandal.

'Sadly, no. The head of home, a woman called Alison Bryant was allowed to quietly leave, getting pay in lieu of notice and she made what looks like a counter-allegation of rape against Mr Atkinson which resulted in his suspension.'

'And was there any basis for this counter-allegation?'

'We don't know. We assumed not because she wouldn't tell either us or the Police what was supposed to have happened.'

'But the whistleblowing was investigated?'

'Unfortunately not. Bryant's word was taken and nothing was done until another social worker made the same allegation which the victim confirmed to the Police.'

Eric Sefton went pale. He was furious. When he spoke it was in very quiet and measured tones. 'So you're telling me a child in our care was reportedly abused by one of our managers, the informant was suspended and we took no action in respect of the abuser?'

''Fraid so.'

'And just to make it worse the suspended informant is not only knowledgeable about employment law, but perfectly capable of speaking up?'

'Uh-huh.' Paula Browne recognised Eric Sefton's anger, but knew him to be fair and reasonable, so he was not going to take it out on her.

'And who was the Human Resources person who advised the manager on that course of action?'

'Actually, HR weren't consulted.'

'Fuck me. You're kidding.'

'No. But I assume the next question you're going to ask is who was the manager, right?'

'Go on.'

'Hilary Campbell, Service Manager, Children's Services.' Paula also knew what was coming next.

'Call her in first thing tomorrow. We'll have to have a suspension and an investigation. And I suppose that because we're dealing with harm to a child, we'll have to pass both names, Campbell and Bryant to the registration body for social workers, - what is it, the General Social Care Council?'

'I'll see to that. Do you want to suspend her yourself, or do you want it done by the Department?'

Eric thought about it for a few seconds. 'No I can't really do it myself. I might have to look later at any possible disciplinary issues depending on what the investigation throws up. Give it back to Children's Services.'

Paula nodded and made her way out.

# Fourteen

*NOTICE OF HEARING OF THE CONDUCT COMMITTEE OF THE GENERAL SOCIAL CARE COUNCIL FOR CONSIDERATION OF A COMPLAINT AGAINST A REGISTERED SOCIAL CARE WORKER*

*NOTICE is hereby given to:*
*The Registrant, Mrs Hilary Honor Campbell*
*7 The Spinney, Redfern Village, Nottinghamshire NG49 7PP*
*Registration Number: 156932*
*and to*
*The General Social Care Council*
*Goldings House, 2 Hay's Lane, London SE1 2HB*
*THAT, following the decision made by the General Social Care Council's Preliminary Proceedings Committee to*

*transfer a complaint against you to the Conduct Committee, a hearing date has now been arranged…*

It was Sunday night. Hilary looked at the letter in front of her which she had received some three months before. The Hearing would be tomorrow. She had already been subject to an Interim Suspension Order and therefore unable to work for the previous eight months. During that time, she had been initially suspended from work, then taken to a disciplinary hearing, where she had been issued with a first and final written warning. She had been off work since then for five months, suffering from stress and depression. The difficulty was that she hadn't done anything wrong, but was accused of leaving a child at risk. It had been Alison Bryant who had actually been guilty, but Hilary felt as if she was having to take the blame. Every social worker knows that once you are hauled up before a Conduct Committee, they will find you guilty and more than likely be removed from the register of social workers.

'Good morning, Mrs Campbell. I'm David Kennison, chair of this Conduct Committee.' A cheery, old-Etonian voice, full of false bonhomie. 'To my right sits Mrs Gladstone, a non-lay member, meaning she is social-work trained and to my left is Mr Armistead. Beyond Mr Armistead is Ms Laidler, our legal representative and beyond her Lesley Boyd our clerk. Ms McNaughton to your right is taking shorthand notes and Mr Jefferson, a solicitor for the GSCC is at the table next to you. Are you represented?'

Hilary was seated in a huge blue-carpeted chamber in the General Chiropractic Council in London. She felt very vulnerable and alone in the huge room opposite the Committee who could end her career. She had to turn up early for the ten o'clock start so as not to risk being late. Hilary never wore a watch. As she told other people, her body electricity would always stop them from working. People had begun to take her seriously after she became a service manager.

She looked across at the committee. The chairman looked like a jovial version of Jabba the Hutt, with his face neck and body seemingly forming one organ.

'No. I couldn't afford a solicitor and I'm not a member of a union or the British Association of Social Workers.'

'Very well.' Jabba shifted on his seat. 'what we will do is first look at findings of fact, eliciting from you what you accept and what you don't accept. We will then go on to look at what issues of misconduct you admit. Following this, we will move to sanction. Is that understood?'

Hilary didn't understand what she should admit as fact and what she should admit as misconduct. They seemed the same to her. She also couldn't understand why she was having the same things for which she had been disciplined considered again. It felt as if she was being tried twice for the same thing. She also felt as if it didn't make any difference what she said. They were going to strike her off anyway.

Hilary was right. The committee did strike her off. It had more to do with the fact that David Kennison disliked social workers than the merits of her case. It wouldn't have mattered what she said and the fact that she had been cruelly misled by Alison Bryant was not an issue of mitigation in which the Committee was interested.

# Fifteen

Daley Stevens opened the white envelope, his hands shaking. 'Auntie Linda, I've got an interview with the Slade School of Art in London.'

Two years had passed since he had moved in with Linda and Charles. He was sitting in the kitchen at the pine table and could not control his excitement. He had had an intense two years, attending sixth form college, working to pass his GCSEs in English and Maths, as well as studying three Advanced Level exams. Linda or Charles worked most nights with him to help him catch up. He was not the most academic of students and knew it was unlikely he would get the three 'Bs' normally required as a minimum for the most prestigious school of art in the country. It had been his art teacher, Nuala Hill who had encouraged him to apply, telling him she had never taught a student with a talent like his for painting, particularly in oils.

He read out loud: 'In exceptional circumstances, a candidate who does not satisfy the above requirements may be admitted to the programme on the recommendation of the Slade Professor and the Tutor to Arts and Humanities Students. On the basis of your submitted portfolio, we are prepared to consider your application and would like to offer you an interview.'

Linda beamed. 'We'll need to change your first name to Lucien if you're successful, or maybe Pablo,' as Charles entered the room.

On hearing, Charles gave a deep booming laugh. Daley always thought that if he ever heard Santa Claus' laugh, it would sound like Charles'. Charles was a broad muscular six-footer, with wire–rimmed spectacles and a big gap in his front teeth. Thirty-two years in the United Kingdom had softened but otherwise very little altered his Californian accent. He had one of those rich brown complexions with a few freckles and was seemingly always happy. Daley had been a welcome addition to his and Linda's home, as, although they would have very much liked children, they had married too late in life for it to be possible. Then, as if by magic, Linda's younger cousin Joanne, to whom Linda bore a striking resemblance, had, through her partner Jake, brought them Daley. Neither Charles nor Linda understood how it worked, but they had sailed through the foster parent approval and Daley fitted in as if he had always been there.

When she had first met Daley, Linda thought he was a desperately sad and lost little boy. During the two years that followed, he'd become confident and developed an inner peace. He was not much interested in going out, idolised Linda and hero-worshipped Charles. He'd also become three inches taller and was, Linda thought, a fabulously handsome young man.

Daley did have a mother, Angela, who would see them when the Social worker visited to review the situation, but did not seem so much interested in Daley as in whether he was, or would become rich. She hinted constantly that Daley should look after his mother with the one or two luxuries she needed. She had no other children, but was six months pregnant. Daley, although he cared what happened to Angela was somewhat dismissive of her pregnancy, saying he would wait to see if the baby arrived. He was very much at home with Charles and Linda and regarded them as his true parents.

On the same day, in the Social Services office, Jake Atkinson, the team manager, approached Sue, the receptionist. Things had changed over the past three years. Frances Phillips had left, as had Lakshmi Patel. Jake Atkinson had been promoted to Frances' team manager post and there were two new social workers, Lloyd and Dev, known as Dave.

Jake continued a previous tradition in the office by instructing that Albert Steggles be dealt with each time he came in. He'd been referred for Adult literacy classes and had moved home, to a Housing Association flat. He would come in once a month, on some pretext, to chat. He had few other people to talk to and he knew all the social workers and liked them. Especially that Sally. She wore short skirts and looked like a film star. And when she smiled at him, he thought all his birthdays had come at once.

Jake smiled. 'Sue, you remember Curtis Wilson, Dolly's boy?'

'Does the Pope wear a silly hat? 'Course I do.'

'He's just phoned me. He's trialling for the County Cricket team today.'

Sue laughed long and loud. 'Didn't I always say he'd make a batsman, or something like that?'

In supervision, Jake sat opposite Tom Davey.

'So, Tom, how are your cases since we've seconded you for three days a week to the union?'

'Of those few I've got, I'm most worried about that Harley Moss.' Tom replied.

'Mother turned up?' Jake asked, expectantly.

'No, nothing like that. We've known nothing of her whereabouts for some two years since the start of the Care Proceedings you did. Harley's fine with his grandparents, David and Susan and mostly very happy.

The only thing is that they're worried about some of his reactions.'

Tom looked at Jake. He was a good manager and Tom felt he could relax with him and speak far more openly than he had been able to with Frances.

'Such as?' Jake pushed a plate of biscuits in Tom's direction and Tom took a Bourbon Cream, dunking it slowly in his tea as he continued,

'Well, he seems to have some sort of phobic reaction to being laid on his back. He panics and cries if they need to do it. He's nearly three and still in nappies, so they have real trouble changing him. It's a recent thing, but they just can't get round it.'

'Phobic's a strong word,' Jake started.

Tom looked across. 'It's a bloody strong reaction. They say it's real panic. I visited them yesterday and Susan lay him on her knee and he screamed. It's unusual.'

'Medical issue?' Jake was quizzical. 'Perhaps you should write to the GP and ask for him to consider specialist referral. It's certainly worth checking out.'

Tom sat still long enough for his Bourbon biscuit to break into his tea. 'Bollocks.'

'Do you remember that time Frances told me off for bad language? Don't you go putting in any grievances about me for damaging your biscuit.'

They both laughed, before Tom looked up, seriously. 'I shouldn't admit this, but you're a lot more knowledgeable than me about grievances and employment law in general. I'm supposed to be the union rep and I have attended their employment courses. If I needed to, would you mind if I picked your brains from time to time? On an anonymous basis, of course.'

'Oh, I don't know that I'm that knowledgeable,' was Jake's response, although he did and he was. 'As long as you don't pick it via the nose, I've no problem with that.' They laughed again.

Tom reflected that the atmosphere had certainly lightened up with Jake's promotion. The work was still tough at times, but the job was worth doing. When you can see visible improvements for the people you work with, it helps you remember why you wanted to be a social worker in the first place.

The door opened. Monica was standing there, a 'guess what gossip I've got' look on her face.

'You'll never guess who I've just seen and where. I was in Ann Summers…'

'Too much information.' Jake's reply was quick.

'Fuck off. Never youse mind why,' tapping the side of her nose.

'That's no way to speak to your esteemed manager.'

Monnie knew Jake wasn't serious. 'Sorry. Fuck off, Boss.' Emphasising the Boss. 'Is that better? Anyway, let me finish. I was in Ann Summers and the manager came through. Do you remember Alison Bryant from Beech Lodge? It was her. She saw me and went back in the office like her fanny was on fire.' Monica turned round, turned back and looking at the plate of biscuits, added, 'And don't finish all the chocolate ones,' before closing the door behind her.

## Sixteen

'Come in and take a seat, Sally.' Jake got up from his desk and sat in one of the four soft chairs in his office round a coffee table. 'Tea, coffee? There are some biscuits and fruit to which you're welcome to help yourself. Let me make a few supervision notes, but before we begin, do you have any items you want to bring to supervision?' He thought for a moment, wondering if he'd seen something in the way Sally was sitting which prompted him to ask, 'Or any informal issues you want to raise with me outside the supervision remit'?

'Tea, please. No sugar.' Sally paused. 'Actually, there are one or two things I feel a bit awkward about and I feel I've got to raise them with you. D'you mind if we do it first and get them over with?' She looked decidedly uncomfortable.

'Nothing I've done, I hope?' Jake moved the plate of biscuits towards her and she took an Oreo and replied,

'Yes, but not exactly anything negative.'

'Go on.'

'You've heard me mention my partner, Gerry?' Sally began to turn a little pink.

'Yes. Is there something wrong with him?'

'No there's nothing wrong.' A minute's silence. 'With her.'

Out of the closet. Good. No problem at all. He would have to make a mental note to prevent any homophobic comments in the team and not to have any negative thoughts about lesbianism himself. She'd kept that well-covered in her time there. Jake wondered if he was the last to know. 'So what have I done?' *Must have been an inappropriate remark. I hope I haven't offended her.*

'Actually, you introduced us.'

'Remind me.' *Do I know any gay women socially?*

'Geraldine's your ex-partner. Oh, God, this is awkward. I wouldn't have told you but with you now being my manager there may be a time you need to visit. And I thought it would be more awkward if you found out by meeting her in that way...' Sally had petered out.

There was a short silence as Jake took the information in. His first reaction was surprise. There had been a time when he had been angry with Geraldine for leaving him in that way and even more angry with the unknown

Sylvia. He briefly thought about his life now and Joanne and realised how well things had worked out for him.

'First let me give you my immediate reaction. I'm very happy for the two of you. I don't have a problem at all with your relationship and I won't tolerate prejudice on the basis of sexual orientation either at work or anywhere else. Incidentally, for your information, I'm over that relationship. I liked her and was shocked when she left me to see someone called Sylvia, but I'm now very happily settled with a woman called Joanne. I just hope Geraldine doesn't feel awkward or make you feel awkward because of our work connection.'

'Gerry speaks highly of you, actually. She felt guilty about leaving you in the way she did, but had to follow her heart. Oh and Sylvia – that's me. Except I insisted on being called Sally since I was sixteen because I didn't like the name. And I wasn't going to shorten my name to Sylly, was I? That would have been…'

'Silly?' Jake interjected. They both laughed.

'So, does anyone else in the team know, or is this to remain a closely guarded secret?'

'That's where it gets complicated.' Sally paused, then continued. 'I think Christine somehow guessed some time back, because she suddenly cold-shouldered me. She avoids me like the plague, leaves the loo if I walk in, doesn't invite me to any of the things she used to. I can't be sure if it's connected, but she seems to have gone right off me. And it's been quite some time now. From before you became our team manager. It makes joint working somewhat uncomfortable. I thought you ought to know. Also, I've made a decision to be open about it now because Gerry and I are going to have a civil ceremony. If I'm going to invite the team to what they'll regard as my wedding, it might come as a bit of a shock if they don't find out until they arrive that I'm a gay woman.'

'Congratulations. Set a date?' Jake meant it sincerely.

'Not yet, but we're thinking about doing it before the end of the year.'

'So, what do you want me to do? Shall I have a gentle word with Chrissie?'

'Thanks Jake. I'd appreciate it. And thanks for being so understanding.'

'No prob. I'll talk to her today.'

Supervision went smoothly after that and Sally left the office two hours later looking positively radiant.

'Christine, could you spare me a moment?'

Christine came into Jake's office and sat down. Almost unthinkingly, he nodded towards the biscuits and she helped herself.

'Have I detected a little tension in the office between you and any other staff?'

Christine liked and trusted Jake. He was a good boss and made sure there was no feeling of working in a blame culture. Since he'd become the team manager, his language was clean as far as she was concerned and his team meetings where allocation was done were always happy affairs. She'd even begun to discuss with him the Sunday-night sermons from the vicar and found he agreed with a lot of the sentiments. He might not actually be a Christian, but he thought and acted like one and that was good enough for Christine.

'There are one or two minor niggles, to tell you the truth.'

'Yes?' As he was asking, Jake poured her a cup of tea. With Chrissie, it had to be a china cup and always milk first. He kept a couple of bone china cups in his office just for her.

'Well, firstly, it's difficult and a bit personal. I know it's me and my fault, but I can't feel comfortable with Muslims.' Chrissie was silent.

'Uh-huh?'

'Well the new guy, Dave. I know he's Asian and I don't like to ask, but…'

'You don't have to. I can tell you Devinder is Sikh, not Muslim. Having said that, I can't encourage prejudice against Muslims. They're just like anybody else. In fact, I understand that Muslims and those like yourself have a common Holy script for the early part. The Holy Koran and the Holy Bible Old Testament are similar as far as Abraham, or as Muslims call him, Ibrahim. So I believe.'

'You're kidding.'

'No Chrissie, go and ask around, or look it up. Do you think it might help you if I sent you on race awareness training? You might find it interesting.'

'Honestly, Jake, I'd love to do that.'

'Righty-ho. I'll sort that one out. But you mentioned one or two things. What else is there?'

Chrissie was quiet for a minute. 'I don't know as it's my place to tell you.'

'Try me. Whatever you have to say might not be new information to me.'

'Okay then. It's Sally.'

'What about Sally?' Jake waited.

'I know it's me again, but I have a real problem with…' Another wait. 'She's lesbian.' Christine was looking very flushed as if it had been a real effort to get the information out.

'I already know that, because she's told me.'

'But what you don't know is that her partner is your ex-girlfriend. And particularly since you've become a manager, I just don't think it's right what with her just sitting there, working for you, pretending…'

Jake interrupted. 'I already know that as well. It's fine by me. It should be fine by you too.'

'How did you find out?' Chrissie couldn't have been more surprised.

'She told me, honestly and openly. And on the subject of pretence, I think that's something you have to discuss with her. I think you'll find her surprisingly open to discussion. But why the apparent distaste? You didn't have a problem before you knew, if I'm correct in supposing you did find out. She's the same person now she was then.'

'It's just you don't know where you stand. The thing they get up to in their private lives – I've seen it in the Air Force and it turns my stomach.'

'Let's unpack this, Chrissie. Have you ever had any hint from her of what she does with her partner in the privacy of her own home?'

'Well, no, but you know it goes on.'

'Has she been in any way lewd, suggestive or anything else in the office that you've found offensive?'

'No.'

'Does she dress or speak offensively in your view?'

'No.'

'Now let's bring it on a little. Do you find me or Tom in any way offensive in terms of the way either of us behaves?'

'No.'

'Do you have any idea which side of the bed either of us prefers to sleep on, or indeed any intimate details of our private lives? I'll bet not. So do you actually know any details of Sally's private life? I'm sure you don't. So what difference should it make which side of the bed she wishes to sleep on and, for that matter, with whom?'

Chrissie thought about that for some time.

'I suppose you're right. It doesn't really make any difference, does it?'

'Go and have a chat with Sally and if you wish, ask Dave about his culture. It can only be a good thing. Oh and…' Jake had had an idea, 'can I allocate you an unusual piece of work?'

'Of course. What did you have in mind?'

'Let's do this properly. I want you to set up a team lunch. If everyone agrees, I'd like you to coordinate a lunchtime one day next week, when everyone will bring in something prepared to eat with the team. Some can bring starters, some a main course or part of a main course and some a dessert. We'll lay aside an extra hour-and-a-half and all eat together. It'll give us an atmosphere in which we can learn to understand each other better. If we're going to work as a team, we'd better become a team. No more than two pounds each and I'll make some dessert, unless Monica wants to make profiteroles, which I know she does particularly well. And no alcohol. Can you do it?'

'I'm right onto it, Captain.'

Jake knew the team lunch would be a success that afternoon as he watched Christine methodically work her way round each member of the team. It was at the team lunch that Sally announced her intention to have a civil ceremony by the end of the year to join her and her partner, Geraldine. And no-one batted an eyelid.

Monica walked into Jake's office and closed the door behind her. 'Can you spare me a few minutes?'

'Of course.' Jake was slightly concerned, as Monica's language on this occasion was so temperate. Usually, in Monica's case this indicated a seriousness to her conversation. She put the paper down that she was carrying in front of Jake. He read the report.

*Yesterday, at the Royal Courts of Justice Court of Appeal Criminal Division, local man Naren Bhargava unsuccessfully sought leave to appeal. He was convicted eighteen months ago on an indictment containing nine counts in all including conspiracy, systematic harassment, rape, causing poison to be administered so as to endanger life and assault occasioning actual bodily harm. He was sentenced to life imprisonment. At the conclusion of the two-hour Hearing, Lord Justice Dawson said, 'We find this appeal holds no real prospect of success. We would add that this is a very serious and unpleasant case and for a man who presents such a danger to those more vulnerable than himself, he should serve a term of no less than twenty-five years.'*

'Do I need to go on? It just goes into what he was originally convicted for, but doesn't name Lakshmi. Just says there were four women victims.'

Jake smiled. 'There's a relief. You can eat your biscuits in relative safety.'

He was a little short of time, as he had several tasks to get on with. However, he was aware that there are only two things any team ever wants from a manager, which are availability and expertise. He tried his level best to give both. His tasks could wait. Monica, having shared the news with him, didn't look about to exit.

'What is it, Monnie?'

'We've made a decision at home. I'm leaving. Pat's moving his business across to France. We're selling up, so I'll have to hand in my three months' notice next week.'

Jake looked hard at his close friend, Monica. They'd worked hard and been through a lot together.

'I shall honestly miss you. Is your bad language up to it in French?'

'Cheeky bastard. To answer straight, no it's not, but I'll teach them.'

She smiled, walked across and kissed him on the cheek. 'You're a good man, Jacob Atkinson. One of the best. You've got that Joanne to look after you and I've no doubt she'll do a brilliant job. When we've moved you'll come and see us, won't you? All three of you.' Jake nodded and Monica left his office.

He rang Joanne to tell her at lunchtime. He would be sad to see Monnie go. Just like the fairy she resembled, she brought a little magic into the office every day. She was one of a kind.

Joanne heard the news and said, 'There's also something I'd like to discuss with you. Two things, actually. Can we meet for lunch, as I'm in your area anyway?'

They went for lunch to Tropical Spice, a local West Indian takeaway and restaurant. While Jake had a portion of curried goat with rice 'n' peas, Joanne had curried mutton.

'Jake,' Joanne seemed hesitant. Jake had a sinking feeling and wondered if their relationship was in any kind of trouble and he hadn't seen it coming. He braced himself.

'Jake, I've been thinking a lot about you and me.'

Shit. It was in trouble. He'd never been as happy in his life as he had been these past two years with Joanne ('don't call me Jo') Cooke.

'And I've got something to say that I don't find easy.'

Please God no.

'I'd like to invite you to move in with me. I'm not normally that forward, but…' and she paused. 'What's wrong? Are those tears?'

'I thought you were going to give me the shove,' Jake stared at his curried goat. 'And there's nothing I dread more. I'd love to move in. Is Amy aware?'

'I've talked it through with Amy and her worry is that you might say no. So was mine and I'd end up looking like a brazen hussy having made a fool of myself. But I need to tell you, hussy or not, I'm in love with you and I want you to be a part of my life.'

Soul mates. Lemon sole mates, Jake thought, remembering their first meeting.

Jake didn't get much work done that afternoon. Joanne didn't go back to work. She'd taken the day off just to see Jake and have that conversation with him.

At half past eight that evening, Jake's home phone rang.

'Mr Atkinson?'

'Yes, can I help you?'

'Mr Jacob Atkinson?' It was a deep male voice. Well educated and friendly. 'My name's Jonathan Turner from Turner Davies solicitors. I believe we have a mutual acquaintance in Lakshmi Patel.'

'Yes.' Carefully.

'She's a close friend and has told me about your involvement during some difficulty in her previous employment. I'm ringing you to ask if you would be interested in coming to see me with a view to applying for a Legal Executive Traineeship, specialising in employment law. If successful, we'll do a salary match to your present job. We would fund you to undertake a course of your choice, either a law degree, a CPE conversion course to law or Legal Executive course. You would end up as a lawyer working for us throughout and for two years after the end of your study. I'd very much like a chat with you. Can you make any time next week?'

Although Jake managed to finish the conversation, he was lost for words when he put down the telephone.

Jonathan Turner put down his cordless phone handset and returned to the leather sofa he had previously been sitting on. He slipped off his shoes before taking a seat and putting his arm round an elegant, slim woman who passed him back his Webb Crystal glass of Barolo.

Putting his arm round her as she snuggled up to him he said, 'I've made the call. I'm interested to see him.'

Lakshmi Patel, shortly to become Lakshmi Turner, gave a half smile. 'You won't regret it, my love.'

She thought back to the darkest period in her life and reflected, 'For every Ravan there's a Ram and for every Duhsasana there's a Krishna.'

'What?'

'I was thinking back to that awful time and then I thought about first meeting you. It means that to counteract every demon there's an angel looking out for you.'

They kissed, slowly.

Sarah Moss walked down North Street onto Fore Street. The sun was shining in Exeter. Finding a chemist's shop, she paused, the final stage of her recent plan about to come to fruition. She was only a fifteen minute walk from home and her former life was little more than a shadow on her memory. At the counter in the chemist, she smiled. 'Have you got any home pregnancy testing kits?'